# Being Saskia
# by
# Rita Trotman

ISBN  9798329165869

For all my grandchildren

## By the same author

Take Three Boys - a memoir set in Romania

Being Kate- a novel

Small Words – a collection of short stories

Nothing Like A Dame – a memoir set in Eton College

Tiger Tails – an illustrated children's book

Wedding Fever - a three-act play

The Elves and the Shoemaker - a pantomime

Cinderella -a pantomime

# BEING SASKIA

## A Novel

# Being Saskia

*When Alfie and Saskia cross social boundaries, the combination of teenage love, drink and drugs turns family life into chaos. Shocked by the action of their children, both mothers struggle to deal with the fallout.*

*Lottie and Tracey were never destined to meet, and each set out on a different pathway to rescue their teenagers from life-threatening situations. However, they have their own perspective on the disastrous liaison, and it appears there are no connective strands.*

## December 1997

Alfie parks his wheels and swaggers to a concrete high-rise where he takes the crumbling steps two at a time. Jeans hang low over narrow hips and a biker jacket protects him from the northerly blow. Nothing athletic ever bothered his pristine baseball boots.

He eyeballs the row of doors on the second floor, on high alert for cameras and snoopers. Satisfied he has no on-lookers, he turns the key on number thirty-two and slips inside.

There's no word of greeting from the old man who's glued to a twenty-inch monitor. The accumulated gloom is bread-pudding thick, and his upholstered chair is scattered with cigarette burns. A whiff of decay marks the man and his possessions.

'Yer up then?'

'Course I am. It's nearly bloody dinnertime.'

Alfie's nose wrinkles at the stench of pee creeping from a glass jar at Dickie's feet. It's the colour of orange juice. Meagre heat seeps from an electric fire accounting for the old man's muffled appearance. His hunkered torso is fattened by layers of clothing which make a robust man of him. Stalactites of mucous perch on elongated nose hair and emaciated fingers worry a duvet wrapped around his lower limbs.

'I delivered that bit of paperwork you gave me.' Alfie runs his finger through layers of dust. 'The snotty tart

1

in the office asked who I was. I told her to mind her own. Jumped up cow.'

 'Spose yer good for something, then. Did yer steam it open? Have a look did yer?'

 'As if.'

Dickie reaches for a match to light his fag. His gnarled hand, peppered with age spots, flicks ash somewhere handy to the ashtray. He's a fifty-fags-a-day bloke with a cough to prove it but nobody suggests he should give them up. He wouldn't give a damn if they did.

Alfie crosses to the window and swishes the curtains back against the wall, allowing new light to lift the gloom.

 'Heh, what yer doing?' Dickie's arms spasm objection. 'I like it dark. Draw them curtains back.'

A solitary tree skitters sunlight into the murk as Alfie opens the window. Wide.

 'Shut that fuckin' window. I'm froze to the marrow 'ere.'

 'Shut it yerself Old Man.' Alfie puts himself in Dickie's face and catches the stench of decay. 'Oh, I forgot. You can't, can yer? Yer legs don't work. Ha! Not such a big man these days, are you?'

The old man mutters about yobs with fuckin' earrings who think they know it all. He gives an exaggerated shiver and hugs himself before lighting the umpteenth fag of the day. He turns up the volume on the television and ignores his visitor who's sizing up the room with an estate agent's nose. 'Good Morning

Britain' adds glamour and volume to the late morning.

'Cut it out Old Man. I've come to visit, haven't I?' Alfie takes command of the remote control. 'Can't hear myself think with them stupid bitches rattling on.'

The old man scowls. 'My tele'.

'Is that your idea of a bit of skirt these days?' Alfie casts a scathing snort. 'At least yer leaving Mum alone, I 'spose.'

The old man's tremor causes the cigarette to dance in his hand. His eyes leak rheumy drips. 'Nobody asked you to fuckin' come. Fuckin' riddles. All you ever talk is fuckin' riddles. Why don't you piss off and leave me in peace?'

'It's Christmas coming up. Want any groceries?'

'Don't want nothing. Christmas don't matter to me. Same as any other day of the year.'

'Please yerself'.

'At least I can still do that.'

Alfie helps himself to a cigarette and lights it with an exaggerated inhalation. He holds the smoke in his respiratory track, revisiting the joy of that first drag after months of abstinence in prison. He blows smoke in the old man's face which heralds a phlegmy cough. 'Better get that cough seen to. Might carry yer off, one of these days.'

'Where's yer manners?'

'Left years ago. Round about the time you crawled into Mum's bed. Got you to thank for having no manners.'

Alfie makes a casual inspection of medical notes sitting in a blue folder. 'On the Social now? Nice. Where's all yer money gone?

'None of yer business.'

'Oh yes, I forgot. You lost it all. Just like you lost yer legs. Very careless letting yobs beat you up in the alley.'

'Shut yer trap. I do alright. And anyway, buy your own bleeding fags. They cost a fortune these days.'

A pack of cigarettes appears on the arm of the chair. 'There you go. Don't say I never give you anything.' Alfie smirks at the pathetic specimen.

'Don't smoke them sort. Time you knew what I smoke.' Dickie picks them up anyway and squirrels them under the duvet.

'Thought I'd keep you company Old Man. What with it being nearly Christmas. Having a turkey this year, are you? I 'spect even an ungrateful shit like you likes a bit of turkey.'

'Pity they didn't leave you to rot inside.'

'Not guilty. Remember? Saskia gave evidence and the judge had to agree I never done it.'

'Says you.'

Alfie sits down on an orange plastic pouffe and faces the breathing bag of bones. 'This is comfy.' He wriggles around to settle his backside.

'That's for me feet, kid.' Arms flap in protest.

'Cantankerous ain't you? I'll not nick it.' Alfie arranges his spider legs around the circumference of the pouffe. 'Comfy.'

'Never mind about comfy. Shut that bleeding window. The sun makes me squint and it's like Siberia in here.'

'Quit carping. You'll soon be nice and toasty, old man. Very soon'

'More bloody riddles. Clear off.'

'I'm going. But you...if I was you...I'd have a nice long sleep.'

Alfie places his glowing cigarette into the surface of the orange pouffe and waits while it melts the plastic. He ruffles the old man's ginger frizz, wishes him Merry Christmas and leaves him to warm up.


## Stutterford Gazette December 18th 1997

Fire officers were called to a flat fire in Western Way on Tuesday where the body of a man was discovered. Mr Richard Hine was overcome by smoke and perished in what officers called a 'strong surge of flames.' The cause of the fire is under investigation, but the disabled man was known to be a heavy smoker. No other occupants in the tower block were injured

***

## April 1997

### Tracey

Whichever way I argued it, bumblebee wasn't a good look. Spindly legs in yellow and black striped tights just didn't cut it on a grown-up. No wonder they were cheap. But while I was sprawling on a dusty floor, they made me look like a puppet with my strings missing. I should have thought more about what I put on that morning. I knew Dickie couldn't stand stripes, nor the clinging yellow jumper, bobbled from too much washing. And my black skirt had risen like a flood tide on the effing Thames; it was right up round me ass. My Alfie would have floored Dickie if he'd found out what he'd done to me.

The row started while I was cleaning Dickie's flat. He'd told me to get a couple of tinnies from the corner shop and I got lippy. It was eleven o'clock already and I hadn't even started hoovering. Anyway, when I was cleaning for him out of the goodness of my heart, I wanted him out from under my feet, not slurping beer around the place. Stupid as I was, I argued and told him to get his own beer.

I'd noticed the twitch of his mouth which usually meant he was angry. He always got a bit red in the face when he was about to blow; his eyes went hard and he sweated over his top lip. I should have clocked it.

He came at me like a raging bull. God knows where an old man stores all that anger, probably the same place he keeps his brains. Wherever it came from, it was quick to spew over, and I took the full force.

I tried to keep my balance when I saw him coming but he knocked me hard then flicked me to one side like I was a bleeding Christmas tree fairy. I bounced off the wall and went down like a sack of spuds. And I forgot to tidy away my skinny legs, even though I knew they aggravated the hell out of him.

'God certainly had a sense of humour when he made you,' he said.

I must have hit the back of my hand on the radiator when I went down 'cos it was bleeding. I sensed him above me, probably admiring his handiwork. He was about six foot and towered like King Kong 'though I could only see his ear and some scraggy hair. But I knew he'd be taking in every miserable detail about me. A bruise was swelling over my left eye, and it felt like it would close. Didn't feel it happen, but guessed it was his fist that did it. My ankle was twisted awkward too and my heart was thumping like I'd run the hundred metres at school.

I glanced at the watch on my wrist. Just to pass the time really as I wasn't going nowhere. Not expecting a number nine bus through any time soon. But my Lily's Mickey Mouse watch made me smile, despite myself. She'd lent it to me when mine gave up the ghost a week or so before 'cos she knew I couldn't afford a new one. Even when the housing benefit came in. 'You'll need it Mum, 'cos you can't be late for work.' She was a bright spark, my little Lily. I took it from her and gave her a hug. Told her she could stay up late and watch TV on the weekend.

Meanwhile, I was wallowing like a helpless minnow on the floor when I should've been trying to get my Alfie out of prison. Dickie's angry face was glowering at me like I was nothing. I snivelled at his feet, afraid to get up. I must have banged me head too 'cos I felt sick, but I tried to ignore it. The whole thing was embarrassing enough for a grown-up mother of two kids, without throwing vomit over his feet.

I squeezed my eyes tight shut 'cos I wouldn't let him see me cry. I hardly ever cried. But Dickie still hadn't moved. He was probably looking at my mousy, short hair which hadn't been washed for days and my ugly face without a smear of makeup. I curled my bitten fingernails into my palms. I 'spose I gave him all the reasons he needed to treat me like shit.

'Just look at you, Trace. Look at you. You're a bloody mess'. He nudged my ribs with his boots which made me gasp. Unfortunately, I caught sight of my reflection in the wardrobe mirror and couldn't argue with him. A pink flush had crept up my neck and something screamed 'loser' in a voice that was louder than Terry Wogan, who was rattling-on in the kitchen.

Maybe wearing something more grown-up might have helped. Perhaps the blue denim dress I'd elbowed away from a yummy mummy in the charity shop would have been better than bumblebee. But I knew I was kidding myself; I'd have been lying at his feet, whatever I wore.

My hand was still bleeding. I eyeballed the blobs of red stuff oozing from a sizeable cut and dared them to multiply. I'd got enough to cope with, without my hand giving in to a pathetic bleed.

He still hadn't moved. His scaggy face stared at me under a cloud of muddy frizz. He usually had a lot more to say, but the lack of a few pints inside him kept him almost civil. His feet were a worry though. A kick in the head wasn't out of the question if I dared move or give him any more lip.

'How do you reckon you're going to help your Alfie? You can barely look after yerself.'

Huh. I'd show him what a mother could do when her kid was in trouble. But it was more than just trouble, wasn't it? My Alfie was in prison.

I wanted to get up. My face itched and I was cold, but I didn't want to risk his number elevens, again. The slime was tight on my skin, a bit like the day they made me run the half-marathon at school, even though I had a letter from Mum to say I had my period. My face was blotched and ugly that day too, I was smeared with sweat, tears of humiliation and the remains of bottled water someone chucked over me. It was meant to cool me down, they said.

It turned out it wasn't sweat, well maybe some and probably lots of snot too, but something else was drying in the mix and I wondered if I'd need a stitch or two.

'Why do you make me do these things Trace? You make me so bloody angry.' Everything made Dickie angry. 'Don't just lie there. Get up you stupid bitch or I'll give you something to really grizzle about'.

I didn't get up, well not straight away, and he never gave me something else to grizzle about. He went to the pub. 'Don't know when you're well off, that's your trouble,' he chucked over his shoulder, like I was listening.

The door slammed and he was gone. I crawled to the chest of drawers and heaved myself up. Everything hurt, including my pride, so I went home. I thought, *bugger his cleaning, he can do it himself.*

Old Man Nesbit was coming down the street on his way to get his pension, but I didn't look at him. I shuffled past and looked the other way. I let myself into my flat and put the kettle on for a cuppa. After a quick grope in the bathroom cabinet for painkillers, I took my cup of tea and crawled into Alfie's bed. It felt safe in Alfie's bed. Who knew when he was likely to want it again? Stuck in that prison, he hadn't been home for weeks and it wasn't right 'cos both me and Lily missed him. Even a tear-away like my Alfie could be missed.

I slipped between Alfie's sheets, gentle so as not to hurt my head. His bed was a tad crusty, and his room was a tip, mostly 'cos he hadn't let me clean it properly for years. He was afraid I'd find his dope. Like I didn't know about his dope? You could smell it out in the hall.

I needed to get Alfie out of that prison, and it was all I could think about. I was convinced he never hurt that girl, but he had no one to speak up for him. Where were all his big-shot friends when he needed them?

My Alfie had been a great little kid, before he went wild. I used to love our teatimes together - it can be a special time for a single Mum. I'd pump him for information about his day. 'What was for dinner then?' He'd huff a bit. 'Dunno. Can't remember.' Mum never asked *me* them sorts of questions. Too busy with her latest bloke, probably. 'Did you play football today then?' 'Aw Mum! It's Thursday. We never play on Thursday'. His little face would screw right up 'cos I'd forgotten his football day.

I used to take Alfie to the park on Saturdays, 'til he was about six. His little legs raced over the grass like a wind-up robot. We used to feed the ducks and kick a football about, and his black curls tumbled over his eyes and his chubby little legs bobbed like a Labrador puppy. I used to dream he could be the next Maradona. Then we wouldn't be living on the bottom rung, would we?

I'd have loved to watch Alfie play games at school like some of the other mums. I'd have hollered at the top of my lungs, 'Go Alfie, go!' The trouble was, I never fitted in with them lot. 'Coon lover' they called me and who was I to deny it with my Alfie like a little milk chocolate drop? I tried once or twice to get into conversation with them, but I skulked away when they kept collaring me about Alfie's antics. 'See this bruise? I'll bruise *his* bleedin' face if he touches my

Ruby again.' And the snotty cow from the hardware shop said, 'I'll have you know my Dan ain't got nits, nor never had. Lying little sod, your Alfie is.'

I sniffed the cold, smelly sheets with more relish than was healthy for a mother, but I could smell my Alfie, and any grain of comfort was welcome. I knew I should have stripped his bed weeks before, but I hadn't been able to do it. And I was glad I hadn't washed my Alfie away. The thought of his clinging scent being washed down the drain was too much to bear. There was more than a grain of comfort to be had in the smell of Alfie.

I kept churning things over, lying in the half-light, but I was none the wiser about what would happen to my Alfie in prison. They took him into custody after problems at his party. Little fool. What was he thinking? Why would he take a girl from that snooty boarding school to his party? As if there weren't enough girls round our way to choose from. I knew no good would come of it when he started doing his painting at that la-de-da college. 'Painting soppy pictures is for playschool,' I told him, but he never listened to me, and see where that got him? They said Alfie stabbed her, but I didn't believe the fuzz. My Alfie was no saint - far from it, but he wasn't a killer, neither.

I tried to sleep but couldn't settle. And even though I was resting, I had to keep an eye on the time 'cos I wanted to be at school when Lily came out. The kids were all I seemed to worry about.

My hand stopped bleeding, but I had one helluva headache. I took more painkillers and decided I'd change Alfie's sheets after all. Now I'd smeared blood on them. I knew I'd regret it, but they were stinking, and it wasn't like he was coming home any time soon.

I was still a bit shook-up, and I must have looked like hell on legs, but my headache had shifted a bit and I didn't feel sick any more. I'd slapped a plaster on my face and knew I should probably have got checked out, but I couldn't be doing with those nurses at A&E who always looked at you like yer were roadkill.

It was pissing with rain - I could hear it on the concrete path outside Alfie's window. I wondered if Dickie would come to babysit Lily later so I could go to work. I hated being nice to him, 'specially after what he'd done to me, but I was all out of choices. After giving Lily her tea, I had my office cleaning job to do.

I always needed money. I was trying to save up for Lily's school trip, and she needed new clothes; her feet grew like an elephant. And I had to manage my money 'cos the Social had got me on their books, and I was never going to let them have a pop at me, not if I could help it.

I knew my face was a mess 'cos I could feel the swelling and one eye had closed. And there was a fuckin' great lump on me forehead. Not that anybody would notice 'cos I'd pull my hoodie up and wait on the other side of the road for Lily, away from the other parents. Later, I'd slip through the streets under my anorak hood so no one would notice me.

The office girls were always goin' home as I arrived. All tits and teeth they were. They giggled like schoolgirls in their smart clothes, whiffing of cheap perfume and makeup. They never gave me so much as a look, but I was worried the caretaker might clock my black eye. He'd want to fuss and send me to hospital and start talking about ringing the nearest woman's refuge. I couldn't be doing with all that.

I had a shower and got some clothes from my room. I wondered if I should let Lily have Alfie's room as he didn't need it. She only had a box room more suited to a gerbil. But that was like saying I'd given up on Alfie, it was as if I thought he'd never come home. I couldn't bring meself to do that. Lily could manage where she was for a while longer.

Alfie had a life all his own. From a young age he went to unknown places with people I never knew. The street kids were cock-of-the-walk around our way and Alfie was top-dog for years. I lost control of him when he didn't need money from me anymore.

I knew I should have asked questions about all his dosh; there was a lot of it, and it couldn't have been legal. But somehow I never found the right time. So, Alfie ran wild from the age of ten. I wasn't much more than a kid myself.

It was a troubled path my Alfie took while he was growing up. I suppose having a thirteen-year-old mother never helped the poor little bugger. Actually I was just fourteen when he was born and Mum agreed to look after him 'til I was sixteen. Then she told me I was on my own. I thought about adoption, but I couldn't have lived with myself if I'd given him away. Mum was all for an abortion, as soon as she knew I was knocked up. I told her to take a running jump.

There was no help to be had from Alfie's father. Tall, dark and lush he was. And married. I couldn't take my eyes off him, and he liked young, blonde girls. Back then I suppose I was jail- bait. I was too young to be doing it and not old enough to know better. As it turned out, he ended up in prison for burglary and never came out. Well, he did come out, but it was in a box. Another inmate was done for his murder, and I didn't want my Alfie to know about that.

Until he was about eight, Alfie always wanted to be with me. Real close we were. But when he got to about nine or ten, things changed. I couldn't put my finger on it, but he sort of grew up overnight. I reckoned it was the crowd he hung about with, older lads who were up to no good. Alfie would come home late and never tell me what he'd been doing. More than once the police brought him home, but he wasn't scared of anybody.

I 'spose, looking back, Alfie worked out a way to do pretty much what he wanted. I was such a lousy mother. I was usually at work and when I wasn't, some bloke was getting my attention. I'd be turning a trick to put food on the table. See, I was no different from my bleeding mother.

My Alfie learnt from a young age the ins and outs of what people did in bed. At first, he asked about the grunting and giggling he heard over the cartoons on TV when I had punters in. Later, curiosity kicked in and he constructed a system of planks and bricks outside my bedroom window. There was no privacy in a ground floor flat. I suppose he was looking for stuff to amuse his mates, but I soon got his measure. Being kids, they couldn't keep quiet, and I clocked them good and proper. The bloke I was with gave me a slap for my trouble and never paid me. I gave Alfie the hiding of his life. I probably should have done it sooner, but it didn't seem to make any difference. He wasn't like his sister who hardly ever needed telling off. But Alfie took the punishment and then put his mind to working out another scam to make a few quid for a bottle of cider and a few fags.

When Old Dickie first tipped up at our house Alfie thought he was a sad old bastard who'd crept round me and wheedled his feet under the table. Alfie had a bit of respect for him at first, but it took a dive as Alfie got older.

Dickie had a flat in 'Skankland' - postal address, Newman Court, which is just around the corner from me. I'd seen him around for most of my life and Mum knew him and never said anything bad about him, so that was something.

I realised Dickie could be a big help when he offered to babysit, 'specially as there was a job going in the corner shop. Lily was too little to leave at home and Mum, true to her word, had washed her hands of us.

And for a while I managed to come off the game. I knew it was bad for the kids to see the goings on, but I needed money, and I was desperate to keep the kids with me; the social were razor-sharp at removing kids round our way.

Dickie's offer to help me seemed the perfect answer. Little did I know he had other plans for me and my Alfie.

***

## April 1997

*Mummy... it was cold... really cold. And there was something wet and sticky on my pink dress. The new one you bought me for Alex's party. I wore it to look grownup for Alfie. I borrowed your lipstick too...the pink one you bought last week. I'm sooo sorry. I know you are really cross.... I want to come home to you and Daddy, but I can't find a way.*

## Lottie

Every morning was a roll-of-the-dice affair after I lost my daughter; roll a six and I'd get up, otherwise I'd languish in bed. Without Saskia, the duvet offered more comfort than a double gin and tonic.

I made deals with myself. If I got dressed by nine I could visit Saskia's room, a pleasure I'd ring-fenced to encourage me to 'buck-up' and insert a degree of normality into my life. Some days it was reward enough to inhale the scent of her, to hug her pillow and forget the wicked night-trolls. Some days the duvet won.

Saskia's bedroom was all I had to cling to when our lives crumbled. Her white polar bear lay exactly where she'd left him, snug on her marshmallow bed. Wisps of stuffing bulged from his belly where she'd over-indulged a bear that was more cuddly dog than carnivore. But when *I* cradled him in my arms, he was miserly and unforgiving; he offered no relief for guilt or pain.

I often heard her voice and knew my delusion made me a fruit cake, but I didn't care. Her crystal tone was always fueled with irritation. *'Knock, Mummy. Please knock when you come in.'*

Sometimes, I opened her wardrobe and gazed at the colour-coordinated clothes. Piles of pink tee shirts, too many dresses and each pair of shoes snuggled in their original boxes. The perfume we gave her was the over-riding scent of my daughter but when I snagged a pink jumper and buried my nose, I dampened the expensive mohair. The sight of her teenage makeup shot arrows of guilt which always found their mark.

I wonder if everyone has an epiphany moment when their lives have been shattered? I don't know exactly how it came about but one day, almost five weeks after we lost her, there was a shift in my head space. I'd already discounted any hope of a happy ending, and I suppose it was my lowest point. The only way was up.

I showered on autopilot which had become my default mode, and slumped downstairs to make a cup of black coffee. And I probably indulged my ability to obsess about Saskia coming home. But unusually, I managed to eat a piece of dry toast with my coffee, grabbed my handbag and car keys and realised I'd made a decision, if not a conscious one. Maybe it wasn't life-changing, but it was certainly the first decision of merit for weeks.

The morning traffic was sluggish. A banging pulse played around my head so I lasered the road and gripped the steering wheel as if it was Alfie Collin's neck. I tuned-in to a bit of Brahms hoping to calm my heart rate. No chance. And I thought about wimping-out, too. I could have turned off the bypass and made for the shops, but my sensible self knew I should keep the appointment. It would please Tom, if nothing else.

Tom was both my husband and best friend, and also the stalwart who had dragged me through the darkest days. He coped with our loss in an orderly and rational manner. Very 'public schoolboy,' my mother said. But when I caught him off-guard, I saw eyes slicked with unshed tears. But much as I wanted to reach out to him, I had nothing in my emotional box-of-tricks to offer.

I parked at the given address, checked my watch and took a deep breath. I'd promised Tom I'd bring an open mind to this appointment, so I ventured forth with my handbag and a good attitude. But intentions can be short lived. Inside the Georgian building my eyes drifted around the blonde wood furniture and designer cushions which were too twee for my taste. The lull of background music jarred. Unreasonably, I wanted to smother the pretty receptionist with her perfect hair and makeup. She didn't even have a bloody wrinkle.

The grey washed walls and framed landscapes were, no doubt intended to soothe, but they didn't soothe me. They reminded me of the art galleries Saskia and I loved to browse. My daughter believed the family coffers to be deeper than they were and often coerced us into buying from any up-and-coming artist who took her fancy. But that fleeting memory of Saskia threatened tears, so I studied the water cooler and counted the stack of plastic cups until I got bored at number twenty-three. The room had all the ambiance of a dentist's waiting room for fruit-loops, and when I passed through the oak door to consult Dr Nancy Edmunds, I knew I'd be one of them.

I picked up a copy of Vogue and my eyes swam across the crowing headline about someone's fantastic life, but I had no appetite for the rich and famous. I discarded the magazine and browsed my own life instead – my happy life with Tom and Saskia. But just when I'd focused on a chubby four-year -old dancing in a field of poppies, the aroma of Columbian coffee hauled me back to reality.

The wrinkle-free eye candy had brought me treats and shamed my petulance with a light-bulb smile. I glanced at the indulgent biscuits with distaste; my stomach threatened to return anything I placed near my mouth. I had as much control over my body as bloody Alice when she tumbled down a rabbit- hole. So, I sipped iced water instead. I realised I was someone who needed mending and a rush of humiliation warmed my neck. I wondered if the clever, highly recommended doctor would emerge and section me.

Too soon her door stood ajar, and sunlight washed the carpet to a rice-pudding smudge. She enticed me inside with the enthusiasm of a party host. From her low-heeled pumps to the silk scarf hugging her over-fifties neck, there was nothing to intimidate. Nancy wasn't paid to intimidate. The air was rinsed with chamomile or maybe rose. Who cared?

I looked around but found no point of reference and wondered why I'd laid myself open to a stranger who'd delve into my life with the stringency of squeezed lemons. And could I expect her to re-balance the strips of matter that used to be me? Probably not. It already felt like a wasted journey.

The life-fixer sashayed across the room and adjusted window blinds to exclude bothering shards of light. The smile that broke through pink lips, didn't reach her eyes.

'So... Lottie. Are you quite comfortable? There's water on the side.'

'Thank you.' I gulped from the glass with gusto usually reserved for a stiff gin. A pair of glass doves on a side table caught my eye. Lalique I guessed. Then a robin in the garden distracted me. I felt guilty for not engaging with the process but for a hundred and ten pounds an hour, I could do what I bloody well liked.

I thought of Tom who was always there for me and wanted this appointment to offer positivity that would lift me from my bleak world. For him it had been easier, at least from my perspective. Soon after we lost Saskia he'd thrown himself back into the rigors of boarding school life. It was unimaginable to me how he could teach history to upper-crust kids when his own child was struggling for life. But when I allowed myself to see the harnessed tears, I knew he was hurting, too.

Tom and I had grown together like Lego. '*A tight fit,*' Mum called us. But he was at a loss to deal with my constant tears and depression. He was caring and in his gauche way would have dunked me in lemonade if he'd thought it would have helped.

Nancy was waiting and I hauled myself into the moment. I sensed it was my turn to speak. But what the hell was I supposed to say?

'Have you ever been in therapy before, Lottie?'

I shook my head with the vigor of someone asked if they smoked pot. Still as a cobra she studied me. I knew she was judging; she'd have noted my lack of makeup, scruffy blue jeans and a linen shirt on its second outing that week. Perhaps my designer handbag lying in a pliable drape at my feet would redeem me. But did I care?

She began writing on rich cream paper which no doubt her clients had paid for. Maybe she was logging that I was stressed. It didn't take rocket science to spot that. She browsed my notes, perhaps checking my age before adding something to her missive. I was a good decade younger than her, but you wouldn't have known it from the road atlas ingrained on my face.

I knew I was scowling, I'd been scowling for weeks, but I didn't care. I knew I was displaying closed body-language, too. She'd have seen it a hundred times before. There was a silence, and I was aware her fees were accruing minute by expensive minute. As someone brought up to appreciate money, I found it hard to squander and the session already felt like an indulgence.

I noticed my file was thin. Not much to show for a family tragedy. Nancy looked up and gave me a smile, presumably to encourage dialogue. But I had no idea what to say. I was a counselling virgin and almost ready to sign off on the project.

After several minutes Nancy gave up on my ability to communicate and tried a gentle nudge.

'How long have you and your family lived at Churchill's College, Lottie?'

I pondered the answer. 'About fourteen years. Saskia was two.'

'Quite an unusual life I should think, caring for all those wealthy boys.'

'We like it.'

Nancy clearly hoped for better. But what did she want? Did she need me to tell her we had a privileged lifestyle? People across the world knew that. I guess I didn't make it easy.

'Would you like to talk about today? How are things today, Lottie? There was no hint of impatience in her voice.

I met her eyes while my brain worked overtime. *Today's crap. Just like yesterday.* I redacted my reply. 'Pretty much like every day since it happened. Rubbish.'

'Mm'.

Clearly 'rubbish' wasn't a technical term she recognised. She pinned me with her professional gaze. 'Have you tried the relaxation methods I recommended in my Notes of Introduction? They can be helpful before your first appointment.'

I gulped at the glass of water like a stranded goldfish and my eyes met hers over the rim. 'Not really.' *Bloody relaxation exercises? Is she kidding?* I obviously wasn't therapy material. Tom had worried it could be too much mumbo-jumbo, and I was beginning to think he was right. But I took a deep breath and tried again. 'Some days I can barely get out of bed,' I offered. 'Hardly conducive to '*doing exercises*', do you think?' I sounded spiky but it was the best I had to offer. And then out of nowhere I felt a wobble coming on. There was something about that place that stripped dignity.

'No. No it's not.' She smiled again, clearly spotting my tear-stained face.

I wondered if the bill was calculated on a points system. Perhaps each smile would claim twenty pounds on the bill. When did I become such a cynic?

'Maybe you're not quite ready.' Nancy maneuvered a seamless change of direction. 'Shall we talk about being kind to yourself? And the need to grieve? Both are crucial in the early days.'

My gaze wandered the room. I was expecting better. Instant gratification would have been nice.

'You need to guard against submerging your feelings, Lottie. You must allow grief to express itself'. Are you able to talk about Saskia - to Tom? To your friends, perhaps? Talking about Saskia is therapeutic. It helps the grieving process.'

'Grieve? How can I grieve for her?' My voice reached several decibels above my usually moderated tone. I gulped a raw sob down my throat which met a knot of anger rising from my stomach. Something threatened to escape and needed containing, for once released it would never climb back in.

Nancy waited. She was paid to wait, wasn't she? Tick, tick. Another thirty pounds.

'Saskia's not dead you know.' I adopted a tone more suited to addressing a child. It was my default mode. 'She's not...anything, is she'. I tried again. 'My beautiful sixteen-year-old daughter is not home where she belongs. I can't reach her... I can't speak to her.' Tears continued to roll down my cheeks expressing decibels of distress.

Nancy offered her sympathetic face. And then suddenly, irrationally, I found Alfie Collings playing hardball with what was left of my brain. I had banned that yob from my headspace weeks before to save my sanity. Bloody Alfie Collings. I even hated the sound of his name. A lad who'd been dragged up by some dead-end family had had the audacity to lure my daughter into his grubby little world. Now, she might never be my Saskia again.

I was livid with myself for crying in front of a therapist. Normally I wouldn't allow such a loss of control. I rummaged in my bag for tissues and found them right at the bottom. They were next to lip balm and my car keys which were attached to a fat, black and white cow with an enormous udder. Mum and Dad had put the key ring in my stocking one Christmas and explained it was for 'the girl who had everything.'

My lovely Dad. He'd thought I'd never get used to 'living with the gentry in that posh school of yours.' But I did. It took a while to meld into the upper-class ways of Churchill's College when my genes were transparently 'farmer's daughter,' but I was supported all the way by Tom, who'd been born to it. He knew all the weird and wonderful routines of Churchill's and took pleasure in my initiation.

Happy as the early years of our marriage had been, they were not fulfilled. Our desire to be parents always sat like a threatening cloud and I never knew when it might rain. The worst times were the early losses of little blobs, too small to be called babies. But they were always babies to me. And then, one day, after years of heartache, everything was perfect. We adopted Saskia and our lives were complete. Except that now, I'd carelessly lost her.

I realised Nancy had spoken and I'd missed it. Again. 'For God's sake,' I heard myself say. I was past caring. 'Grieving is for the dead. Well, it is in our family.' I swallowed hard, searching for a straw of dignity. 'She's not dead. My Saskia's not dead.'

'Grieving comes in many forms, Lottie,' the paid-to-be-patient Nancy offered.

I noticed the strands of grey at her temples and wondered when she'd get her roots done. Her voice took on a softer timbre. 'You've suffered loss, Lottie, even though Saskia is still with us. Loss of your daughter as you knew her.' She sat in silence while I digested her wisdom.

I remembered to breathe. 'I've hardly cried. Not properly...until now. I've been too bloody angry to cry.' I knew I sounded pathetic, but it was the best I could do.

Nancy remained silent and watched as tears escaped from a deep, dark place. It was an expensive session If I could only cry and shout. I never shouted. I rarely cried. But maybe this woman had no idea what being in a coma was like. '*Well tell her then Snooks.*' I could sense Tom urging me on.

'She's poked full of plastic tubes,' I began. 'She's fed through a tube, she pees through a tube and she's breathing courtesy of a machine.'

Nothing was forthcoming from the counsellor, and I wasn't sure if I could carry on. The pain was palpable and my breathing short and shallow. I managed to knit a few more words together. 'Saskia is alive, but only because other people choose it.' I dabbed at errant tears. 'What if they decide to switch off her life-support?' I'd strung together ten little words and crumpled with the agony; I bled from their very formation.

Nancy nodded her understanding and indicated a box of tissues beside me. I heard a whine and found it came from my own mouth. 'Tom's getting on with his life and I can't bear that,' I bleated like a three-year-old who'd lost their sweets. I thought of Tom who was teaching a group of over-privileged boys at that precise moment, none of whom had slipped into a coma in the last few weeks. 'It makes me so angry,' I told Nancy. 'Unreasonably angry.' I gulped and tried to grab a semblance of self-respect.

'It's Tom's way of coping, Lottie. He probably needs to be busy. That's how some men cope with trauma. Do you and Tom talk about Saskia? About your hopes for her future? It's important that you keep talking to each other.'

'We do, when he's at home but everything seems so, I don't know, tense. Everything makes me angry.' I caught the contents of my nose with a tissue taken from the box on the glass coffee table. In that environment 'man sized' would have done a better job. I failed to harness an unattractive sniff or rein in the raging emotions and still little of value was forthcoming from the counsellor. The bill was escalating minute by expensive minute.

'She slipped out to meet this...this yob who enticed her to a party. It was a drug-fueled party and that's why I'm so angry. She knew better.'

Nancy watched me struggle.

'And there's the guilt. I didn't know what she was up to.' I wiped more mucous from my face. 'I'm her mother. I'm supposed to know. I'm supposed to keep her safe.'

Nancy waited. I had no idea what she was waiting for. Until I completely broke down? There was another silence.

'Mothering isn't a perfect science Lottie. And piling guilt onto unhappiness is never fruitful. Anyone can be deceived by teenagers. They specialise in covering their tracks.'

I was beginning to wonder if that was it. Was that the sum total of what I could expect from the clever Nancy? 'Anyone can be deceived by teenagers?'

'Do you know what? I don't need this.' I had no idea where it sprang from. 'I can talk to myself at home, thank you. And for free.' I grabbed my handbag and left the room as mumbled apologies dripped into soggy tissues.

'Send my husband the bill,' I threw at the Receptionist. I walked out to threatening skies and I hadn't even brought an umbrella.

***

## Tracey

Alfie's antics started when he was about eight and started throwing stones at the empty factory off Claymore Street. A gang of them used to hop over the wall where the topping stones had slipped and once they were inside, they'd take bets on who could smash the most windows with bricks they found lying around the site.

The following year he took up with some older boys who used to nick petrol out of cars. At first, he just stood lookout. He told me he used to keep an eye out for the fuzz. After a bit, the gang let him try his hand and told him to suck on the plastic pipe they'd dropped into the tank of an old, beat-up van. What they didn't tell him was that he had to stop sucking just before the fuel hit his throat; it was nothing to them, but my Alfie nearly choked to death. They laughed their socks off, apparently. 'It was a bit like giving a blowjob,' he told me years later. After that, I think the gang decided to promote him and he became a little thug who was afraid of nothing and no one.

I didn't clock it for ages, but Old Dickie had started giving money to Alfie. I noticed it on his fourteenth birthday when a crisp fiver was shoved under the tomato ketchup like it had a purpose. I thought it was a present. What I never knew was what went on after I left for work that day.

'There's a little job I need doing', Old Dickie told him when he saw Alfie eyeball the note.

'Oh yeh? Legs can't get you to the shop to buy your ciggies I 'spose?

'No. Not as simple as that'.

'Spit it out then. A fiver would be better in my pocket than yours, Old Man'.

'Less of your lip, Nipper. That's if you want to get yerself a regular little earner'.

'I ain't got all day, Dickie'.

'Just like yer mother you are. Impatient. Can't wait for nothing, you.'

'Yeh, Yeh.'

'Well, it's a bit delicate.' Dickie gave his nose a conniving tap. 'Sort of...man-stuff. Think you're up to man's stuff? Keep yer gob shut can yer'?

'Try me'.

I'd have rung Dickie's scrawny neck if I'd heard the dirty old man talking to my Alfie like that. But what could I do? Dickie already had me on the game. I knew I should've gone to the Social or the police even, but I was ...sort of in it before I knew it and Dickie always told me they'd take my kids away if I dobbed him in.

At fourteen my Alfie should have been out playing football, not taking filthy money from Dickie. That's prostitution of the worst kind in my book. Using kids. But my Alfie loved it 'cos he'd never had so much money in his life. It was more than I ever seemed to have. And that's how Alfie got away from me; he never needed anything from me after that.

A recurring theme with my Alfie was him asking who his dad was. 'Load of good for nothing', I told him when he asked. 'Not worth the shirt he stood up in'. My mum used words like that. Obviously, Alfie knew his dad was brown or black, he knew that by just looking in the mirror. He used to tell me, 'I don't care if he's a wanker, at least he'll be *my* wanker if you tell me who it is.' It was heart breaking. How could I tell him his dad was knifed to death in prison ten years before? He had so much hope in those brown eyes that I didn't have the heart to tell him.

'Does he live round here then?'

'No'.

'How did you meet him then?'

'Never you mind'.

He told me that sometimes he used to pretend the school bus driver was his Dad. He'd imagine waiting 'til all the kids got off the bus and then he'd say, 'Oy mate, I'm yer kid'. He'd have liked a dad who was a bus driver. Actually, I used to think anybody real would have done. Well, anybody except a copper. He couldn't imagine having a dad who turned out to be a copper, could he? But Alfie made no headway with me and eventually stopped asking.

When he got the hang of girls, he didn't think it was all it was cracked up to be. The local girls were mostly slappers who were hell bent on getting pregnant to get a council flat. They'd think nothing of dropping their pants and leaning on the wall behind the youth club. I knew how it worked 'cos I'd been one of them. That's how Alfie came along, and I had to leave school to have him.

I tried to make Alfie want more than I'd had. He always said he didn't want to be tied down with a slapper and a kid, and I hoped he meant it. Not that I thought he'd get it on with a girl from that posh college. Her mother should have known better than letting her loose on my Alfie. Enough to turn a boy's head, wasn't it?

Alfie used to tell me snippets of what went on with the street gangs, if he was in a good mood. 'How do you know when a Murton slag has an orgasm? She drops her pasty!' Alfie said the lads never failed to find that one funny. The Murton Estate was full of 'quick fix girls' and my Alfie soon got bored with them. But then he found a posh girl and ended up in bloody prison. He'd have been better tied with a Murton slag and a kid, wouldn't he?

When he was coming up seventeen my Alfie had a chance to make something of his life, or so I thought, at first. The volunteer do-gooder at the youth club fell over the fact that he could slap a bit of paint on a canvas. I don't think Alfie cut her much slack to begin with, but she kept admiring what she called his 'free spirit with a brush' until she won him over. The 'winning-over' was little more than an exchange of a few words, from what I could gather. The do-gooder encouraged him and found a bit of money to pay for all his paint.

Out of the blue, the youth worker arranged for him to paint in the local posh college art room. It was only once a week to start with although I noticed Alfie soon started going more often. He couldn't go in if la-de-da parents were visiting nor during exam periods, other than that he could go pretty much when he liked as long as he signed the visitor's book and marked himself out when he left. Bet they loved having an estate kid around. Made all of them stuck up pricks feel good, I 'spect.

I met the twit of a volunteer who arranged it all while I was shopping in Tesco. She was sweeping around the meat section like someone who'd escaped from the local pantomime. She left her trolley and galloped across when she saw me, even 'tho I tried to nip behind the cereals. It was embarrassing. She told me in a posh, loud voice, 'Alfie has blossomed within the hallowed walls of Churchill's College.' *'Blossomed,'* my ass. I just hoped that while he was sitting in la de da land, he'd remember it was only four short miles from Skankland. We both knew that the only reason he was allowed in to paint was to do with the Government's idea of *'giving the underclass a bit of a go'*. But he seemed to like it, and I hoped he would change his lifestyle. He was definitely seeing less of the hoodlums but, of course, it turned out he was shagging that girl.

Alfie told me the college boys all thought his art was good. If he was in a good mood he'd sit with a cup of coffee and tell me all about it. He could take off their plummy accents like he was born to it and used to make me laugh 'til I cried. I could never imagine him in that school. But he liked people telling him he was talented; he liked the fact they found some good in him. Who wouldn't like a bit of praise now and then? Especially as he wasn't used to it.

He told me about one college lad who wasn't a stuck-up little prick. Bertie, he was called, and he painted similar stuff to Alfie. 'You're really good', Bertie told him without a bite of sarcasm. 'I wish I could capture that raw, street-quality.'

'I live it. That's why it looks real. Thing is, I can't imagine having an Old Man who'd send me here.'

'And I can't imagine having all that freedom either. Can you really stay out all night without having to tell your Mum? Doesn't she worry?'

'Naw. She knows I can look out for myself'.'

But did I? It broke my heart when he told me things like that. Brought home what a lousy mother I'd been.


My Lily always came out of school like a ray of sunshine. Unlike her brother she loved learning. I'd put off telling her about Alfie being in prison and luckily, she was at school when they arrested him.

But she'd already asked why he wasn't home. We were used to him disappearing for a few days, but this was a bit too long. I worried some kid would tell her at school, so I decided to tell her myself when we had tea. I bought two big sticky buns 'cos she loved them and hoped it would soften the blow when she heard about her big brother.

I sometimes thought all Alfie's problems started when Lily was born. He was nine at the time and I guess he was jealous. One day I caught him nearly throttling her and he said, 'I'm just loving her Mum. She'll laugh in a minute.' I knew to be a bit more careful after that.

When I was growing up, I'd heard people say, 'there's no such thing as a free dinner,' and that one came home to roost soon after old Dickie appeared on the scene. After about two months of getting to know him, it started with, 'let me put the kettle on love, you look parched.' He'd sit me down like I was the Queen and make me a cup of tea, more often than not with a Hobnob to dunk.

'A bit of sympathy goes a long way', I'd heard Mum say more than once and Old Dickie was good at tea and sympathy. To be honest, I didn't really notice him wheedling his way in, but before I knew it I'd had a door key cut and he was popping in just when he was needed, and often when he wasn't.

Alfie had been a latch key kid, but I wanted better for Lily. I'd promised myself I'd try to be home when school finished. Sometimes I made her a ham and salad cream sandwich or even a bit of home-made cake. I was learning all the time.

I had to admit Old Dickie turned out to be a Godsend in the beginning. If I couldn't meet Lily from school then he was the next best thing, and Lily liked him. He seemed OK with her, so it worked for all of us. Not that she was a difficult kid. Not like Alfie. She always wanted to please which saved one hell of a lot of grief, especially after bringing up Alfie.

Thinking back, it was probably just the odd touch in a doorway that started it. A sort of 'sorry' as Old Dickie brushed past me. But it soon became obvious it was deliberate. I could have told Mum, but I'd thought she'd overreact and face him up about it. Then I'd have no sitter for Lily 'cos Mum wouldn't give up her comings and goings to babysit for me.

He was old enough to be my grandfather. God, that sounded bleak when you put it like that. I preferred to think we were both needy. You know, both of us needing somebody for a bit of a cuddle. I asked myself what difference age made anyway. He wasn't revolting. Just old. In need of a good steam iron when he took his clothes off but, hey, beggars couldn't be choosers back then.

I never thought of myself as lovable, I never had the looks. But if some lonely old man who liked my kids wanted to give me a quick shag now and then, where was the harm in that? And it *was* a quick shag, too.

One day he showed me a picture of himself in some sort of soldier's uniform taken when he was about twenty. National Service, he said, whatever that was.

After that I found it helped the shags along a bit if I pictured him during his better days. Quite handsome he was. It passed the time when I imagined him in his heyday, as he called it. 'All the girls fell over themselves to go dancing with me,' he told me. 'Right light on me feet I was.'

But he wasn't very bloody light on his feet when I knew him, though I got used to his finger-wagging routine to coax me onto his lap. I'd have liked a dad who did that. I'd wanted one who read me stories at bedtime and felt all whiskery. But after I'd sat on Dickie's lap for a while, he'd heave his arthritic joints out of the chair and take me along to the bedroom where he'd collapse with a groan onto his back. 'Spose he was lucky to still get it up at his age, but it isn't exactly 'a cake with a cherry on the top', as Mum would have said. But I got good at it and in fairness, it never took long. He was a noisy bugger 'tho, and more than once I had to slap his Y fronts over his mouth to shut him up. He had nosy neighbours. I hated gossip from the neighbours.

I remember I'd been trying to save up to take Lily to the Zoo. She loved animals and I'd been promising for ages that we'd go. I was still short by quite a few quid when Dickie said, 'have a few crisp ones from me, it's just a little something to help get you there this side of Christmas.' Cheeky sod, I thought 'cos I was funny like that. I never liked to take charity off anyone. But he'd said it in front of Lily, so what could I do? And we had a cracking day out. I even squeezed a cheap tea out of the money as well. Lily was well happy.

Soon after that came what Dickie called a 'business proposition'. It went something like this; *'everybody has something they're good at, and you, my little pigeon pie, are a bloody good shag. If you've got a talent, then you should use it to make a bob or two'.*

He'd got it all worked out. He'd be in my flat with Lily while I used his old people's flat or 'Sheltered Housing' as he liked to call it at Skankland. I'd be doing what I was *'good at'* and share the money with a man old enough to know better. He'd convinced me no one would suspect. 'Who would think you were carrying on in sheltered housing? They'd think you're in there doing a bit of cleaning.' At least it would be safe, I thought, and my hours at the corner shop had just been cut. Money was tight as hell, and I wanted my Lily to have everything I never had. Mondays and Thursdays the 'arrangement' was gonna be at first, with men supplied by Old Dickie. 'They better be clean,' I told him. 'And none of that kinky stuff.'

\*\*\*

*Mummy, I don't think Alfie was pleased to see me at his party... even though it took a lot of arranging so that you wouldn't find out. I'm very sleepy Mummy but I need to tell you things...Alfie was different when I got there... He didn't look after me like I thought he would, and I didn't know anybody. I didn't...fit in. They were all very... noisy. And they stared at me as if I was an alien. And then a boy, well, a man really, came up and offered me a cigarette. I said no thank you, but he placed it between my lips and said, 'chill little girl, take a puff of this and you'll feel great.'*

## Lottie

Tom wasn't best pleased when I told him about my visit to the illustrious Nancy; he looked seriously annoyed, and I caught a flash of disappointment. But eventually he laughed. 'I can imagine the scene Snooks. I did wonder if Dr Nancy Edmunds was ready for Lottie Hanson.' He chuckled so much that even I could see the funny side, eventually. 'Oh Snooks, you need to give it at least one more try. Nancy comes with tip-top credentials.' So, in his inimitable Tom-like way he persuaded me to ring and apologise and have another go. I made an appointment for the following week, although I had no idea what it would achieve.

The days slipped by in abject misery. Guilt mounted over the late starts I made most mornings, and I found it hard to focus on anything without Saskia around. I missed her unladylike habit of whistling which drove Tom wild, but I would have given anything to have heard her whistle, just once. She'd recently started searching through my wardrobe. She 'borrowed' things that weren't considered 'too Mumsie' and that included my precious L'eau de Issey perfume. She'd become obsessed with her appearance, which concerned me, but my friend Ursula told me it was normal for a girl of sixteen. But all I could remember about being that age was wearing jeans and helping Dad with the cows. I certainly wasn't chasing boys.

My inactivity was beginning to make me feel old and useless. Too often I heart-searched and found countless flaws in my ability to mother a child. I'd allowed our daughter to get stabbed and mixed up with drugs. That snagged at my heart, especially as we were so close. I thought she could confide in me, tell me anything. How naive was that?

I scoured my brain for anything that could have flagged up her liaison with that yob during the weeks leading up to the party. I had to admit she'd been a little distant, but I'd put it down to hormones. Everyone told me it was normal for a sixteen-year-old girl to be secretive. As my experience of childcare was limited to boys who were simple enough, I took advice and let her work through whatever was happening inside her head. Only it wasn't happening inside her head was it? With hindsight, I knew why she hadn't been communicating with us and Alfie Collins had a lot to answer for. He'd driven a mechanical shovel through my very being.

I constantly felt wretched. Every day my hair was caught back in a fat sleeping plait, and I looked about seventy. Grey hairs were prominently intermingled with the red and I knew, in another life, it would be time to start colouring them. But not at that moment. I hadn't even washed it for a week.

I heard Enid, my daily, bumping around the kitchen. Tom was long-gone to his classroom and although I was full of good intent to get up and have breakfast with him one morning, it wasn't on the agenda that day.

I showered and made it to the kitchen but didn't fancy any breakfast.

'Morning Mrs Hanson. It's nice to see you up.'

From anyone else it would have sounded like sarcasm, but not from Enid. She was the most loyal person I knew and was already hard at it on her knees, fumbling under the dresser with dexterity no woman her age should possess. I winced as I thought about her knees on the limestone tiles, but she was oblivious.

'Good morning Enid. I'm up but not sure I'm functioning.'

'Baby-steps. That's what you need. Baby-steps. Good job those boys are off home for a couple of weeks. Give you a bit of a rest.'

'You're right,' I appeased her. 'But we've had to cancel our holiday in Cornwall. Everything is so uncertain. It'll be the first year Saskia's missed her beach holiday in Sennen since she was two.'

'You can make up for it when she's better. She'll love a little holiday when she wakes up.' She dived to clean a mark off the floor. I knew she struggled to manage our family's trauma too, almost as much as we did.

I pondered her wisdom but wondered if we would ever again take Saskia to our haven in Sennen. It was the place where Tom could always unwind from a busy term, but it felt a million miles away. I struggled to recall the sensation of feet on powdery sand, and I couldn't smell the ozone that defined the Cornish village for us.

'I picked your cream skirt up from the dry cleaners on my way in. It's still got a stain right on the front.' Enid rose from her knees, gaining purchase on the kitchen table before she leaned her ample body across it. 'I'll take it back when I go home, and they can do it again. For free.' She pushed her glasses up her nose.

We were so lucky to have Enid working for us. She was devoted to Tom and Saskia, and I reaped the benefits of her kindness, too. She'd been a backbone to the family since...well, forever it seemed, but especially while Saskia was in hospital.

'Thanks for that'. I didn't care a jot about my cream skirt. I couldn't even remember when I'd last worn it. Dear Enid. She tried her best to keep body and soul together for us.

'Shall I...' Enid hesitated and I knew what was coming, 'give the pink room a do?'

'Not today Enid.' I was sharper than she deserved but it was the best I could do. No one would touch Saskia's room until I was ready. I needed to spend time there while her scent still lingered. I didn't want to smell furniture polish instead of Saskia. I liked to hug her collection of fluffy dogs and her darling Casper Bear, and I knew he'd be the first thing she'd want when she woke. Everything was just where she'd left it, pristine and colour-coordinated. My daughter had a very precise eye for such things which she certainly didn't get from me. More likely from - but who knew where an adopted child got their traits? If it's from nurture then Tom took the credit. My scatty lifestyle drove him nuts at times.

I softened my reply. 'Not today, thanks. I'll put some coffee on and I'll call when it's ready.' I couldn't imagine a day when I'd say, *'Enid, give my daughter's room a good spring clean, would you? Bundle up her clothes and I'll pop them down to the charity shop.'* I had to believe she'd come home. I knew all the textbook stuff about moving on at my own pace, and I knew there were no rights or wrongs for dealing with trauma. I had a master's degree in counsellor speak. But no one would violate Saskia's room. Not yet. Not until we were out of options.

I nibbled on a piece of toast and noticed the view through the Victorian sash windows was, as always, stunning. No matter what time of year, the view was always beautiful, and I was filled with gratitude for the lifestyle I'd been gifted. I never tired of those Wimbledon-perfect lawns and the brimming, colour laden borders. That spring they were themed in blues and yellows and were heart-achingly lovely, although I realised I hadn't noticed them as often as I should. In fact, I was ashamed to admit I hadn't achieved anything for weeks. The catastrophe with Saskia had created a maelstrom of hurt that was raw and smarting and never seemed to draw breath; that was on the good days. On bad days I felt as if I was bleeding inside. Those were the days when a physical pain enveloped me; those were the duvet days. I found the 'not knowing' what the future held, was the real killer.

Day after miserable day I continued to dissect our parenting skills, or lack of them, which filled many hours with misgivings. Our first mistake, I decided, was giving Saskia our complete trust and I hated to ask the question, but had we both been too busy with the boys and the business of term-time to notice what she was up to? Fifty boys under our pastoral care were a heavy load which we shared, and both enjoyed. Most of the time. Tom could be forgiven as he had a massive workload at school, but I should have known something was going on. I knew I'd never forgive myself.

I put the coffee on to perk and stared out of the window. Maybe if I concentrate on something beautiful it might change our lives. I frequently recalled the long and tedious road we'd travelled to adopt our beautiful child, and now I'd thrown her away. And I felt such an idiot. I'd let her slip through my fingers.

Tom and I had spent years on the 'baby treadmill,' trying to produce a longed-for child, before we finally conceded defeat. 'Sometimes there's no good reason why you can't conceive,' the best physician known to man told us, all those years ago. 'You're both healthy individuals but it isn't happening for you.' Cold comfort was how I viewed his wisdom. And, if I'm honest, we were tired of making love to order. Following temperature charts and checking dates took all the spontaneity out of our sex life.

We had several unsuccessful attempts at IVF which cost a fortune, but more importantly, left me feeling like a pin cushion packed with useless hormones. Tom, for whatever reason, felt less than the man he wanted to be. It surprised me that trying to get pregnant became such a burden, especially as friends were dropping babies like confetti. I thought I'd have an emotional melt-down if another friend asked us to be godparents to their new arrival. Eventually, we gave up the fight and faced the monumental process of adoption.

It took months and months of parent training classes and the indignity of strangers delving into our intimate lives, before a tussle headed two-year-old became 'available for adoption'. Issues were raised about Saskia's first two years of life with her birth family. The social worker explained they ranged from child neglect to questions about sexual interference, all of which I preferred to bury deeper than Tutankhamun's tomb. Considering her difficult start in life, it was a miracle she'd grown into such a competent, beautiful young woman and it filled my heart to bursting. When I thought of her lying in a coma, it filled my heart so full of tears I feared it would break.

We brought Saskia to Churchill's when she was two. The finalising of her adoption coincided with Tom's new post as house master which felt like the icing on the cake. After long years spent in the desert of childlessness, it was the most exciting and perfect time in our marriage.

Having Saskia helped me make friends at Churchill's. There were plenty of mothers with children on campus, many ensconced there by ambitious husbands striving to excel in their profession. For many years I'd avoided women with children to stave off the heartache, but it felt different when Saskia arrived - I felt as if I fitted in, and I found friendship, too. And for Tom, who was living and working in his alma mater, life continued to rotate on a solid axis.

Saskia was a cheeky, red-headed little angel with freckles and a cute smile, and she enchanted us like nothing had before. Tom and I were obsessed with her. We checked on her in the middle of the night to be sure she was breathing, and she wasn't allowed even close to a nut for fear of allergy. Her arrival thrilled my Mum and Dad too and I was almost as happy for them as I was for us.

Now, fourteen years later, all I wanted was to spend as much time as possible at the hospital with our princess. I watched her for hours while she slept, and Tom visited whenever he had a spare minute. I took fresh clothes for her and a bundle of optimism each day. I even took the perfume we'd given her at Christmas because a nurse told us scent could be evocative. We were desperate to give anything a try.

I used to paint her nails, usually something soft and pink to match her dresses. I chose deep red when I dressed her in leggings. I wanted her to look her best when she woke because she'd never forgive me if I'd allowed her to become a mess while she slept. How

Saskia looked was paramount to her day and I wasn't going to be found wanting in that department.

I talked to her and held her hand while she slept. 'She may be able to hear you,' the doctor told us when she was admitted. 'Talk to her as if she's awake. No one knows for sure what she hears.' So, I told her how much she was loved. I told her that we weren't cross with her, even though we were. I told her how well her tummy had healed but I didn't tell her about the ugly scar the knife had left in her abdomen. And I told her to wake up so that we could take her home.

I'd been daydreaming again and suddenly noticed the coffee was ready. I called Enid and poured a large mug for me and a smaller one for Enid who was caffeine conscious. Buck up Lottie Hanson, I told myself. Enough self-pity.

'Shall I boil you an egg Mrs Hanson? Nice and soft, just the way you like 'em?'

'No thanks Enid. I've tried a piece of toast. Coffee will do for now. Don't let yours get cold.

'I'll just empty the bin. Give it time to cool down.' She chuckled in her inimitable way. 'I looked in the fridge,' she told me as she shook out a new bin-liner. 'Seems like there's a bit of out-of-date food in there. Shall I chuck it?'

'Thanks.' I felt a tingle of embarrassment. Wasn't that the sign of a slovenly housewife? We didn't eat much during those dark weeks and I knew Mum would have frowned upon my wastefulness.

We sat in companionable silence until Enid told me she'd decided to spring-clean the sitting room. I was never totally comfortable having daily help, but Enid was wrapped inside the package of privileges that came as standard for a Housemaster at Churchill's. She came alongside the delivery of wines and spirits we received each term, our family food allowance and our daily newspapers. In addition to Enid, we had an odd-job man and a chef who not only fed the boys, but our family too. It was hard to stay in touch with reality when you lived at Churchill's.

I was staring into the dregs of my coffee which had already gone cold. And I could sense the energy being expelled by Enid as she moved furniture and hoovered next door. She appeared to have the strength of two men, and nothing was ever too menial for her. Jolly Enid's face always suggested she was deeply privileged to clear up other folk's grime and dirt. Scrubbing around our walk-in shower and popping her head down someone's loo came as second nature. She was avidly loyal to Churchill College and all who sailed in her. And she was kind too. Over the last few weeks, she'd knitted Saskia a family of pink rabbits which she thought would match her pink bedroom. 'She'll love 'em Mrs Hanson. You see if she don't?' I secretly thought Saskia would hate them, but I'd ensure Enid's feelings weren't hurt when Saskia woke up.

I loved the boys we cared for - some more than others, but they all had something to commend them even if you had to search for it. I spent years entertaining boys to afternoon tea in our home, usually half a dozen at a time on Sundays. They used to devour my chocolate cake as if they'd not seen food for a week, always ably assisted by my daughter. Most weekends I'd arrange a video night to make boarding school feel more like home and Saskia was always to be found in the middle of the fun. She'd learned at an early age how to manipulate the male of the species.

As the boys got older, I taught the keen ones to cook. 'It's a great way to impress girls,' I'd tease them. 'If you can throw together a spag bol, you can't fail.' I usually sat with them after cooking and joined in their banter as they scoffed the product of their labour. 'An honorary chap', they called me. 'Not like staff and not like mothers.' I liked that and I never regretted the mountain of washing up they created. Every pot and pan were caked in sauce and strings of cheese clung to my Crown Derby. Never having a son of my own, I developed a special rapport with the boys.

Tom had an entirely different, more disciplined relationship with them, and had reason to admonish me on more than one occasion for what he pompously called my 'over familiarity.'

 'You can't tell them that winning games doesn't matter. Not in this establishment,' he said peevishly after our boys lost the final of the inter-house Rugby Cup. It all seemed so pointless to me, sending boys out on wet, freezing afternoons to wrestle the hell out of each other in the name of ball games. Who cared who won? But I learned to keep my thoughts to myself, and my mouth tightly zipped. Over the years, the fragrance of money and the twang of upper crust England honed me into something resembling a good House Master's wife. I learned to stand on the touch line and call for success of the team in dulcet, lady-like tones.

Enid bumbled into the kitchen which moved me to action. I glanced at the clock and felt ashamed when I saw it was past eleven. I should have rung Ursula and asked her over for coffee, but I hadn't. I'd been neglectful of my social circle. Friends were supportive of Saskia's plight, but none of them really understood the pain of talking to an unresponsive daughter who lay with closed eyes.

The worst thing about our daughter's coma was that however hard you searched, there was never anything to hold on to. Nothing indicated she'd ever come back. Not a flicker showed on her beautiful face and eventually you imagined the worst. How could you not?

I noticed my diary on the dresser and realised I was in breach of promise. Nancy had asked me to keep a diary. It would help me measure how things improved – well that was the theory. But most days I had no idea what to write so I didn't write anything. I could have written, *feel like shit...again. Cleaned teeth.* I'm sure Nancy would have considered that a lack of effort on my part.

I put my coffee mug in the dishwasher. I could see boys playing rugby in Nether Field which adjoined the far corner of our garden. Their voices filtered across the lawns, 'Pass it. Pass it here.' In many ways, the boys at Churchill's had quelled my longing to have more children of my own. I'd have loved a houseful if they had come our way, but it wasn't to be, and we learned to be satisfied with one beautiful daughter. Optimistic people had told us that after adopting a child, hormones often kick in and a natural pregnancy could follow. But it wasn't to be for us.

Over the years, the ache for more babies calmed itself. I became a realist and threw myself into my role as Tom's support. Churchill's College taught me to applaud every success of the boys in our house and smile with delight as I presented trophies to the talented. And I learned to be amusing and witty when asked to host dinner parties or entertain parents. Most of all, I made my own parents proud. Dad told anyone who'd listen about his successful daughter and her '*life with the nobs*.' Bet that went down well at Cirencester cattle market.

Enid appeared and plonked her backside on a kitchen chair. She put her feather duster on the table. 'That lad's grandmother plays bingo on Tuesdays'.

I realised I was holding my breath. I knew Enid was always to be found at bingo on Tuesdays and struggled to absorb the implication. 'Are you sure?'

'Sure. I'm sure. From what I know of them they're not much of a family. Rough as rats.'

'Do you think she knows you work for us?' I failed to quell palpitations and reached for a glass of water.

'Not from me she don't. Wouldn't be seen dead talking to the likes of her.' Enid wandered off to her cleaning after turning Tom's radio from Radio Four to something offering music she could sing along to.

I smiled despite my misery. I reasoned the link with Alfie Collins was tenuous, but it made me nervous.

***

*Mummy, the man who'd been nice to me was suddenly horrid, he wanted...sex. I could feel his hand up my dress and he was fumbling in my knickers. I was so scared. He had a knife and threatened to cut me if I refused. I was petrified. He...he pushed me down on a pile of coats and put his hand over my mouth - I could hardly breath and I was afraid to move. There was someone's black leather jacket near my head. I hated the smell...*

## Lottie

The trips to hospital were difficult; every single day we mustered courage to face the barrage of medical equipment that beeped, ticked and seeped fluid in and out of Saskia's body. It was an unnatural world. It was hard and clinical but somewhere amongst it all, lay our daughter. Life was full of conflict. Every visit was a reminder of that bastard's violation of our daughter as we came face to face with the damage he'd inflicted on her perfect body. And yet seeing her also eased the heartache, if only for a short while.

Caring for the bodily needs of my sleeping daughter was the only practical thing I could offer. I fed her through a tube and watched as the milky fluid disappeared to nourish her from within. I washed and changed her as if she was a baby again, only now she had none of the feistiness of her infant-self. I longed for her to tell me her nail polish was the wrong colour or she hated to wear trousers. And yet in my heart I knew it may never happen again. Our lives were charged with conflict and contradiction.

Being near Saskia had that amniotic pull all mothers feel, and for hours I'd stare deeply into her pretty face and pray for a sign of change. I made deals with God. I held her hands, which were warm and living and felt just like our old Saskia. But she wasn't there.

It was several weeks into the trauma before I could begin to unpick the details from that night when Saskia had slipped out of our sight, full of lust and deceit. I eventually understood the logistics of how she did it. She'd involved one of the boys in the House to cover for her, which made Tom mad as hell. But I told myself all the sneaking about and the lies were in the past, and no matter how much we wanted to change it, we couldn't.

After weeks of resentment and uncertainty I reached the point where, more important than anger and blame, was the need to have my daughter back home. I longed for her to open her eyes; I wanted assurance that she wasn't brain damaged. I reasoned, if Saskia had lost the use of her legs, I'd have spent every waking hour helping her to walk again. I'd have driven her on to greater achievement. And I'd have believed she could do it. But this was in a different league. Day after day there was no sign of improvement. There was nothing real or imagined that could tell us Saskia was still inside her body.

If getting up in the morning was an achievement, then I made progress. I wrote in the famous diary and gave myself a pat on the back for small steps of progress. 'Have a plan for the day, however small. Have a reason to get up,' were the words of wisdom from clever Nancy. Saskia was my *raison d'etre*. I knew all the theory of dealing with the tragedy, but I struggled to put it into practice.

How the hell Tom managed to get up each morning to deal with the demands of adolescent boys was beyond me. I knew it was unreasonable to be angry with him, but my anger had a habit of firing pellets at those I loved best. Some days I accused Tom of not feeling the pain that crippled me. I knew it was spiteful. I think I harboured some unreasonable fear that I might lose him, too. Then I'd be alone. Those words echoed like a mantra.

My pathetic loss of confidence felt like my alter ego. I was unfamiliar with being a wimp and it was hard to find any normality in my life. But how *could* life be normal without Saskia? 'Men cope differently,' the clever counsellor told me with monotonous regularity. 'They feel things in a different way and getting back to work is a coping mechanism.' Yeh, right. Maybe I needed some of that.

I sometimes played the 'what if' game. It was pointless, but I had so much time on my hands. 'What if,' Tom had chosen a grammar school for his teaching career instead of this snooty public school? 'What if,' we weren't living in a goldfish bowl, (or rather, a cut-glass champagne flute?) 'What if,' our family life wasn't planted in the echelons of money and power? If Tom had chosen a teaching job in a comprehensive school, we'd have lived in a normal house, had normal friends.

I daydreamed about Tom coming home every evening around five, carrying bundles of marking, asking what's for supper and checking on Saskia's homework. So, was it all Tom's fault then? Not a conclusion I could support. It was too easy to lay blame, and I tried hard not to do it.

Some days Tom and I hardly spoke and some days I gave myself a stern talking to. However much I wished Tom had taken a different career path, when I reflected on our lives I had to be honest and admit I too had learnt to enjoy the cloistered environment of public-school life. I knew the privilege of money and education had undoubtedly softened both of us, and I appreciated that we lived an extraordinary life.

An unimaginable burden was dumped on Tom, ten years into our marriage. Saskia had already arrived, and we were absorbed with a tumbling three-year-old and living our perfect lives when the blow fell. It was unexpected and devastating. Tom's elder brother, Piers, died in a car accident. And as if losing his big brother wasn't enough, Piers was also his best buddy and his soulmate as well as heir to the family estate and title. As second born son, Tom had been shooed into the world to make his own way. Suddenly, amidst all the sadness, there was expectation he'd put aside his loathing for the estate, which included his widowed mother, and pick up the responsibilities. There was another life waiting in the wings and like the sword of Damocles, it threatened our happiness.

I tried to support Tom during those crippling months, but what he needed most was his brother back in his life. I allowed myself to assume our lives at Churchill's were over and steeled myself for the inevitable lifestyle change. I knew the pressure Tom would be under to satisfy the wishes of his mother.

Tom's inheritance was an impressive pile. We spent a couple of Christmases there when we were first married but our visits were fewer than they might have been. His relationship with his mother blighted Tom's desire to spend time in his childhood home and it was a regret he never came to terms with.

But eventually I was happy for my assumption to be proved wrong and also full of admiration for Tom's grit and single-mindedness. He stamped his foot firmly on the soil of inheritance and money and announced he wasn't up for the responsibility of the estate and certainly not the care of his ailing mother.

'Piers knew I never wanted the estate. He always encouraged me to follow my own career,' he told his mother. This I knew to be correct, but circumstances had taken such an acute turn, I feared family honour would melt Tom's resolve. But it didn't.

After a gut-wrenching funeral to lay his brother to rest in the family crypt, Tom risked the wrath of his mother by declining to step into his brother's shoes. The title came to Tom regardless, although he vowed never to use it. The Cotswold pile and three hundred acres of land with its corresponding overheads, was also his.

Tom's mother was the deciding factor when he chose to stay at Churchill's. Neither of us could envisage running the estate while she was alive. The Old Dame, as I called my mother-in-law from hell, lived on the estate and had never accepted her second son's decision to teach at Churchill's. I once heard her mutter, 'we didn't spend money on your education for you to become *just* a teacher. And why on earth did you marry a girl from nothing?' She really was a ghastly old lady. 'Her head's up her ass,' as my dad so daintily put it.

It was agreed, after much posturing from his mother, that a cousin would run the estate until such time as Tom 'came to his senses'. He was passionate about educating young minds and spurring on successful teenagers; his heart was patently in teaching. When he took his first-class honours degree to his alma mater, he knew he'd found his niche in life.

I had a fledgling career of my own during our early years together and had found it hard to forfeit my dreams. My hypothetical kicking and screaming was how I remember my behaviour when we moved to Churchill's, which was far removed from the life I wanted. I didn't want to live amongst wealth and power and the feisty girl I was, made sure Tom knew it.

I was acutely aware that Tom's move to Churchill's would eradicate my ambition to make my parents proud of me. To reward them for all their sacrifices. From the time I was a small girl I'd believed that I would be the space scientist who changed the world. I'd already spent a few years working with a company in Oxford who were involved in space programmes, and I'd been offered my dream job in America just when Tom popped the question. I loved him and reasoned my career would be put on the backburner anyhow when our clutch of children arrived. So, I reasoned Tom deserved my support although it was given without generosity.

Tom's employment package at Churchill's included a perfect little cottage within the grounds for us to live in. I was going to play at house for the first time. I listened to Mum's homely advice which was something along the lines of always putting a cooked meal on the table when he got home and keeping him warm at night. With this firmly dismissed as '*old hat*', I set out to make a success of my new life in my own way.

Making a home and supporting my husband in an alien world was tough. But we did enjoy cosy evenings, eating delicious food and drinking copious amounts of Merlot. And we made love with the vigour of youth believing it was simply a matter of time before starting a family. We thought having babies was a given.

The long school holidays were a delight, and we travelled far and wide, mostly to the Far East. We also spent happy times with my parents in the Cotswolds. Tom had never known a real family and I encouraged him to share mine.

I was thrown off-kilter by the opulence of Churchill's College and awed by the grandeur and ceremony which everyone except me took for granted. As new arrivals, we were dragged around drinks parties and shown off at raucous dinners. I always felt we were being scrutinised and judged, and many years later, when my feet were well imbedded in the hallowed ground, I knew this to be true. It was for that reason I always tried to put new staff at ease and never forgot my own baptism by fire.

However, we obviously passed muster, as eventually Tom was offered the post of Housemaster and we plonked ourselves into an entirely new adventure. The new house was large enough to contain fifty boys and had a stunning apartment for us which laid claim to the garden side of the house.

I realised I was living the life Tom had been raised to and I loved him enough to grasp it and claim it as my own. I settled into my destiny with much stern talking to myself and many tears, but eventually I became happy with my lot. And at times I positively loved it.

Saskia's coma cast detrimental shadows in every corner of my life. I asked myself if I would always gaze at teenagers in the street, seeking out Saskia's sea-green eyes. Would stunning red hair under a shaft of sunlight always make my heart skip a beat? And for how long would I steal into College Chapel and kneel in prayer as if I believed in a higher God? Was it an example of what the clever counsellor called a 'coping mechanism?' Maybe I'd started coping without knowing it. That was a bright thought for the day. Get it in the bloody diary!

Tom and I enjoyed a lifestyle which was unusual by most people's standards. Firstly, we shared our daily routine with the twelve hundred schoolboys of Churchill's College. Here, princes and titles were as common as frogspawn in the boating lake and for two thirds of every year our family lived under the same roof as fifty of the little darlings. I knew their smell, their dirty little ways and their vulnerabilities. Being a Housemaster's wife could be tricky, although I think I shaped up pretty well.

Saskia's coma affected the boys too. They were so sweet when they knocked on our apartment door and brought gifts for her. I hadn't the heart to tell them nothing would go to the hospital until she woke. Tom said, 'let's keep everything in her room until she comes home, then she'll know how much she was missed.'

Privacy in our personal life during term time was defined by an exhausting half hour chat in bed at night and, before we lost Saskia, a chat over a cup of morning tea. While dealing with Saskia's coma, however, I wished I was a million miles away from the opulent lifestyle that sucks in the gullible and impersonates real life. I had days when I wanted to run home to my parents, to be a child again, to be cared for and have no responsibilities. But the reality was my lovely parents had no idea how to help.

My best friend Fiona in Australia offered to fly over when she heard about Saskia. But I didn't think even she could help. We'd been lifelong friends and understood each other like sisters. I'd have given anything for her to wrap her arms around me. But she was busy with four kids and a sheep rancher husband, and I couldn't drag her all that way just to see me blub like a baby over her alpaca jumper.

I had friends in college, too. There was a handful of wives and daughters of the establishment who were somewhere on my wavelength. They tried to be kind and called me regularly for updates, but this was mostly something Tom and I had to bear alone. We were too exhausted to discuss possible outcomes, and the division between us widened.

***

**Tracey**

I went to see my Alfie in that miserable prison. It took two bus rides to get there and looked like the heavens were about to open while I was waiting for my connection.

I found my way in with other people off the bus and I eventually joined a queue. After about twenty minutes and nothing happening, a bloke in a long overcoat started gobbing-off, 'How much longer have we got to wait?' When nobody answered he got beside himself and used some ripe language and ended up being marched off by the screws. I sympathised with him 'cos it was like the staff were on a go-slow. I dug my ID from me bag, ready for my turn at the check-in and waited. I just waited. The officer was a miserable cow; she never smiled once. You needed yer visiting order and a photo ID to get in and she looked like she hoped I'd forgotten mine.

Annie Etheridge told me not to eyeball anybody during the visit 'cos then nobody can pick a fight. I couldn't see anybody likely to do that. There was a posh old couple behind me and all they kept talking about was 'when, Anthony was little'. Yeh well...all our sons were easy when they were little.

The sniffer dog took no notice of me as I passed through to the Visit's Hall, thank goodness. I worried I might smell of cannabis from Alfie's room. I looked around and it was like being in a huge porta-cabin. It's a bit like an aircraft shed, I thought. And I could see my Alfie sitting at a table wearing a bright yellow waistcoat. I wanted to hug him but knew better. Instead, he gave me a wink like there was nothing to worry about. It didn't take me more than a couple of seconds to see it was a false front he was putting on.

He looked sad and thin and all the swagger had gone out of him. At first, he just stared out of the window but when he studied me with those chocolate eyes of his, I had to lie about me bruises as Dickie's handywork had barely begun to fade. I think I got away with it.

He asked about Lily, and I told him how well her reading was coming on. She was a whole year ahead according to her report. But Alfie was agitated. I knew my son well and he couldn't hide stuff from me. I pushed him a bit. I tried to get him to talk to me about prison 'cos I hoped it would help him cope. And when he started, it poured out like beer from a bottle. Most of what he said was more than I wanted to hear. He looked a sad little shrimp, and he'd been told he could be facing an eight-year stretch.

He didn't give that girl drugs and he didn't knife her. 'I love her Mum. I love her.' I asked him if he didn't do it, then who did? I reckoned he had to know. He thought about it a bit, like he was trying to get a story right in his head. He said she was with an older bloke who gate-crashed his party. I asked him who and he said everyone knew him as Zillon. But they'd found Alfie's prints on the knife so that made him a little liar, didn't it?

I'd got a few details about the state of the girl from Annie Etheridge who lives near some woman who works for the family. Apparently, the girl was close to death by the time the police arrived, and everyone had scarpered, including my Alfie. The girl was found lying under coats and old curtains. I asked him why he'd run if he didn't do nothing, but he never answered. The trouble was, all the kids were programmed from a young age to scarper when the fuzz arrived, but that still didn't excuse him for leaving a girl to die. Alfie said he never realised how serious it was. Must have wanted his eyes tested, I told him. He tried to get her home to me, he said, but apparently, she wouldn't move.

After a few minutes of silence he asked if I'd heard how the girl was. 'Saskia Mum. She's called Saskia and I love her'. I told him I hadn't heard anything for the last week. I wanted to change the subject. I knew if she died, he'd be done for murder.

'What's it like in here?' I asked him.

'It's shit and likely to get a lot worse. New regulations come in next week,' he told me. 'No more fags allowed, even in our cells. Some of the blokes are going nuts.' He frowned. 'We're an experiment, apparently. They want to try it out on us before other prisons have the same shit piled on them.'

I thought about the consequences of taking away a prisoner's fags. It seemed barbaric to me. My Alfie loved his ciggies and he'd be stuffed without them.

'As if it ain't bad enough in 'ere. They want to give us chewing gum – like that'll help.'

I told him to give it a try 'cos I knew a couple of people who'd managed to give up smoking by chewing special gum. But he wasn't listening. All he kept on about was his cell. I 'spose that's all he'd seen since he came in.

'I lie on my bunk and stare at the ceiling most of the time. I can see where some filthy buggers have spat gob and gum up there. Looks like the Milky Way if you have a bit of imagination.'

I had to laugh 'cos if there's one thing my Alfie had it was imagination.

'Only way to pass the time is looking at the ceiling,' he said.

It seemed bloody grim to me.

'Even remand prisoners like me don't get perks,' he blurted. 'It makes no difference 'cos the rules are the same as if you've been found guilty. And the thing is, I never did it, Mum. I might have given Saskia vodka, but I never went near any E's and I never stabbed her. I tried to get the knife off the bloke and it went into Saskia instead. I love her. She's the best thing that's happened to me so why would I? But nobody believes me.'

I wondered to myself why that would be. 'Any news on the court case yet?'

'Should be soon. Because I'm remanded I might jump the queue. I cost them too much to keep.' He chuckled but I could tell it was false.

I noticed a small boy in the Visits Hall showing his dad a drawing. It made my heart lurch and took me back a few years to a place I preferred not to remember. Alfie never had that advantage 'cos I refused to bring him inside to see his dad. I started thinking I might have made the wrong decision.

The time went really quick – well it did for me. I had an urge to put my hand over my Alfie's and tell him I'd sort it. Just like when he was a kid. But I couldn't sort it, could I? After what felt like ten minutes but was actually nearly an hour, I looked at Lily's Mickey Mouse watch and realised I'd miss my bus if I didn't go. Alfie let me give him a hug, but his body was stiff as a board. I knew he was scared, and it broke my heart.

All the way home I tried to come up with a plan to get Alfie out. Why weren't the police looking for this other bloke? Too many questions and no answers did my head in. I felt useless and that's a bad feeling for a mother when her kid's in trouble. I thought about going to the local nick and telling them about this other bloke. Not much point, I decided.

I got off the bus just in time to fetch Lily from school and I needed to tell her I'd been to see her brother. She loved him, but I wanted Lily to have a better chance in life than I'd managed to provide for Alfie. My Lily was bright. She had a real chance to make something of herself, except now she'd got a jailbird for a brother.

I spotted Mum waiting by the school gate. She was in a leopard-print tee shirt with sparkles that made you wish you were wearing sunglasses, and striped trousers that looked like pyjamas. I was embarrassed.

'I told you I'd fetch her.' I was a bit sharp, but it didn't matter with Mum.

'I know. I wanted to make sure you'd be back.'

'Course I am. Why wouldn't I be?'

'Yeah, why wouldn't you be? Every day yer visit yer son in the nick, I 'spose?'

'Don't need sympathy. Just need everybody to mind their own.'

'I just wanted to help. You know.'

'No, I don't know. Bit late in the day fer motherly concern, don't yer think?

She stomped off muttering about ungrateful kids.

When Lily and I got home Old Dickie was on the doorstep. 'Spose I should have been pleased he was offering to have Lily while I went to work, but I wanted to smash his face in for how he'd treated me. I was still full of anger and it was all bottled up like fizzy pop.

'Seen the lad have you?'

My bruises had come out like a rainbow and I wanted to slam the door in his stupid face and smash his nose. See how he liked being hurt. But I didn't and he followed me indoors.

'I'll put the kettle on and then your little princess can tell me what she's been up to at school.'

Lily smiled at him like he was Father Christmas. I could have killed her.

I found a biscuit and told Lily to go and tidy her room. Then I turned on Dickie. 'Alfie's going to plead not guilty.' I noticed his weasel face was a bit scrunched-up like he was thinking. That'd be a first.

'Hmm. Did his brief tell him to do that?'

'No. He says he never done it, so he won't plead guilty.'

'Could get less time inside, if he coughs to it.'

'But he's not going to cough if he never done it.'

'Don't look good is what I'm thinking. No witnesses are going to talk from what I've heard. No witnesses can be as bad as too many. Know what I mean?'

I did know what he meant. It was easier to fit Alfie up than do much digging around. That's what he meant. Tick box exercise for the fuzz.

'Course, if I could sort out a witness to say Alfie never done it...well, it would be a whole different ball game, wouldn't it?

I allowed my heart to do a little flip at the thought of Alfie coming home but then I remembered who was holding the carrot and forgot it. 'Yeh right. Who'd be daft enough to do that then?'

Dickie tapped his nose. 'You leave it to me. Just leave that to me.'

Like I was holding my breath. Dickie never did anything for me fer nothing and he wasn't going to start now.

I made Lily a jam sandwich and told her she could watch telly. I was hoping she wouldn't notice there wasn't much food for tea. Sometimes, on jam sandwich days we played princess tea party 'cos she always chose jam then. Princesses must like it.

I gave Dickie a cup of tea, more from habit than anything. I could hear him asking Lily about school while I was getting ready fer work. I never worried - not exactly, but I hoped Dickie wouldn't do anything to my daughter. Not like he had to Alfie. But she was still so little, and I told myself he wouldn't be interested in her. Only the worst kind of pervert would have touched my Lily.

\*\*\*

*Mummy, I'm still trying, honestly, I am... but I can't wake up. I keep thinking about that horrible man and why didn't Alfie do something? I know I screamed a lot but... I was so frightened the knife would slip. It was touching the skin on my throat and his other hand was inside my knickers. I remember thinking... he couldn't...you know...get inside me with only one hand free. And I was right Mummy...he couldn't get inside me because I wriggled and bit him and screamed and he couldn't...you know...do it. Alfie must have seen what was happening because he started to fight the man to get him off me, but I don't think he saw the knife. And suddenly I had unbearable pain. I remember how I couldn't breathe 'cos they were both so heavy...It really, really hurt.*

## Lottie

One morning when I'd made it downstairs at a reasonable hour, I looked at the kitchen notice board hanging above the toaster and then wished I hadn't. 'The Bursar invites you.' I mused over the sub text;

*the dinosaur's pad calls us to mingle with a dozen or so sparkling members of Churchill's College for the dreaded drinks party*. And it was that evening. Could I face it? Was this the time to re-enter Churchill's society after weeks of abstinence?

I decided to visit Saskia earlier than usual that day while trying to muster courage to go with Tom to the soiree. He'd done so much on his own and I knew he'd appreciate the effort. I talked myself into going all the way to the hospital.

Most days I helped with Saskia's personal care. I washed her and had learnt from the nurses how to keep her mouth clean. I moisturised her skin with my best Chanel hand cream and brushed her hair which still held its lustre, despite her sleeping state.

A lovely Thai nurse who always greeted us with a beaming smile popped her head around the door. 'Good morning, Ping, I don't suppose there's any change?' I asked. I knew there couldn't be, but I always asked.

'Nothing today Mrs Hanson. But we all hope for good news.'

Hmm...I negotiated all the tubes attached to Saskia and took her cardigan off by rolling her gently towards me. I put it on the chair. She was in joggers and a blouse which were easy to dispose of as I took her in my arms and told her that today the sun was shining, and we all wanted her home. I changed her pants and eased her gently onto her mattress. When she was first admitted I'd asked the sewing department at school to open the seams of her blouses, tee shirts and dresses on the side her tubes were attached and they put Velcro fastenings on to make the dressing process easy. It worked a treat.

'Can you manage?' Staff Nurse appeared. 'Here. Let me help.'

Saskia looked so pretty in pink. I put her soft ballet pumps on her perfect feet and gazed at her.

'There's always hope, you know.' Staff nurse was trying to cheer me up and I smiled to reward her.

'I know. But hope runs a bit thin, sometimes.'

'I'll make you a cup of tea Mrs Hanson. Are you expecting your husband?'

'No. He won't make it today.'

She disappeared while I held Saskia's hand and fought the tears.

'I brought your perfume darling. I'm going to make you so fragrant all the medical students will want to date you. I'll spray your hair too.'

I painted her nails and told her all the news from home. I told her a funny story about the new boy Anderson who was trying to climb out of the dorm window when a prefect caught him and pulled the sash window down so hard that he wriggled like a little piglet.

I was just about to tell my daughter how lovely the garden was looking when there was a loud beep which scared me half to death. I was momentarily frozen until I saw a nurse open the door. She quickly discovered the ripple mattress had stopped its constant wave of motion and expertly un-plugged and then re-plugged it. There was an immediate quiet, but it took some time for my racing heartbeat to calm. 'I thought Saskia was having a heart attack,' I told the nurse through dry lips. But then I saw her body continue its gentle undulation which assured me all the mechanics were working again.

'I might as well turn her now that I'm here. Doesn't she smell lovely. Sorry if I smudged her nails,' she said, noticing my bottle of nail varnish.

'It's no problem. It was dry.'

'Nice colour. It matches her dress. Makes a change for her to wear a dress, doesn't it.'

'I thought so. She's a real girlie-girl and I'm fed up with her joggers and tops. I want her looking nice when...'

'Of course you do.'

'There'll be hell to pay if she wakes up and looks a mess.'

'I'll bet. Remember to keep talking to her Mrs Hanson. You never know... you might trigger something positive.'

I wondered if Saskia's adoption details were in her notes. Would anyone think them relevant? Did people point fingers at adoptive families when things went wrong? I had never considered there to be any essence of 'nature' in our daughter, only 'nurture', but common sense told me there had to be both. When Saskia's adoption was finalised, no birth-mother access was requested and secretly, we were relieved. We knew her father was heavily into drugs but had no indication that her mother indulged.

The details of how, when and where we would tell our daughter she was adopted had been teased apart and reassembled until it was a sleek manuscript of love and responsibility. Every relevant book on Waterstone's shelves was digested to ensure we were sensitive and qualified adoptive parents; we didn't anticipate any hiccups. The social worker warned us that sometimes the big revelation doesn't go according to plan but we both thought that wasn't likely to happen in our family.

We decided Saskia would be told while having our summer holiday in Sennen, the year that she turned eight. Being on holiday was always the happiest and most relaxed time of the year so why not tell her while sifting powder-white sand through our toes on a sunny day? If Saskia asked, and we doubted she would, we could truthfully tell her we had few details of her birthparents. But when the moment presented itself, we were collecting shells and set for a picnic on the beach. Tom broke the news of her heritage using the words we'd rehearsed a thousand times, and I was right, Saskia had very little to say. She took the revelation in her stride and visibly warmed to the sound of being 'chosen'. But soon, even that became boring and the subject was dropped.

How could life go on as normal? I could not equate the sleeping girl with our feisty daughter. She'd lost weight, hadn't had a period since it happened, and her skin had become translucent. But the nurses told me these changes were not unusual. 'Trauma,' they said. I thought an awful lot was being passed off as 'trauma'. Nothing made sense. I had no idea how those bodily functions related, if at all, to hope for Saskia's future.

The nurses and doctors were friendly and professional, and we couldn't have wished for better care for our daughter. But there was no hope of healing for ourselves while she was still damaged. No one can prepare you for the mental tightrope walked when a loved one falls into a coma; it was like walking on glass or through the fires of hell with no guarantee of reward.

It was Saskia's mental state I feared for most. Her team told us the CT and MRI scans showed no sign of permanent damage, so why didn't she wake up? And would our exuberant daughter be a vegetable if she did? The anguish of those words left holes in my heart.

I longed to get my hands on the little shit who'd damaged her; I knew I'd have squeezed the life from him. I used to lie awake at night and torture myself while the sound of a gently ticking clock taunted me. I was choked with anger over Alfie Collins. What on earth did Saskia see in him? My beautiful girl, who could have had any boy she wanted, had to choose him. I couldn't make sense of it.

Tom told me he met Collins once in the college Art Room. He explained what the lad was doing there and how the art master considered him a talented lad. Tom even bought one of his bloody paintings, no doubt encouraged by Saskia. At least I had the satisfaction of taking a Stanley knife to that 'so-called art' and shredding it beyond recognition. It was immensely satisfying at the time, although I recognised it as a childish act.

Tom told me the boy had pale coffee skin, long curly hair and Celtic eyes. Attractive, he said. I tried not to imagine him touching my daughter's perfect body. Did he take her virginity? I was under no illusion that the relationship was a meeting of minds. However, when the doctor told us there was no evidence of sexual intercourse that fateful night, it held a morsel of comfort.

And of course, alongside everything else life had thrown at us, we had to deal with her deceit. She broke our trust and there was no other way to say it. She knew we would ban her from seeing a yob like Alfie Collins, so she didn't tell us. Simple. God, I was angry. I kept asking myself if Saskia had thrown away her life on a drug-crazed youth who would hopefully end up in prison for a very long time. But his demise wouldn't bring Saskia back to us, would it?

Strangely enough the daytime could be worse than the nights. I seemed to wear a gut-wrenching sense of loss like a second skin during daylight hours. I missed our daughter's energy in the house; we used to laugh at the most ridiculous things. Saskia could see humour in anything and often she poked fun at the academia that surrounded our lives. She could mimic the headmaster to perfection and even Tom was not safe from her wicked humour. I softly admonished her, as a mother should, and then laughed at her very joie de vivre. She stopped me becoming saturated with snooty people and their stuffy traditions. Tom despaired of us. He rarely saw the joke, bless him.

The police told us a date had been set for the court case. I couldn't believe we would be spending August in court instead of in our beloved Cornwall. Our time there was always special, but there was no chance we'd walk on the soft sandy beaches, feel wind in our hair or dip our toes in the azure waters. Not for the foreseeable future.

I agonised about Saskia taking drugs – I knew this was the real nitty gritty of her coma. And it was hard to grasp that my baby girl had experienced something even Tom and I had no knowledge of. Did she pop a pill, or did she smoke something? Did she know what she was doing or was she forced? When the toxicology report came back, however, we knew she'd taken amphetamines of dubious origin; she'd also smoked pot and drunk a considerable amount of vodka.

The police told us there had been a spate of problem drugs around the area and they suspected she had fallen victim to a 'bad batch'. This made her coma all the more worrying for us. And we knew every detail of that fateful night would become public knowledge in court, then picked like crab meat from the shell by the press.

Saskia had been given all the drug awareness it was possible to instill in a child. She lived with a father who was drug-savvy and vigilante; nothing mattered more to him than to keep the boys in his house safe. Talking about drugs in our home was open and honest and she'd had a no-holds-barred explanation of the perils of taking them. She should have known better; she did know better.

But the worst of it wasn't the drugs or the booze, it was the knife that ripped her open. Why was she mixing with someone who'd put a knife in her? How could we grasp that concept? Did she refuse him sex? Was sex at the bottom of it all?

Tom and I summoned every last strand of courage in readiness to hear Collins talk his way out of what he'd done. We were told he intended to plead not guilty, so we were forced to face him at a trial. And where were we supposed to find the strength for that?

If I was going to make it to the drinks bash, I knew I'd have to buck up. I plugged in my hot brush and dug out the summer sandals I'd bought in Madeira. I shaved my legs and painted my nails and thought the diary was going to be so full of improvement it might go up in smoke. It made me smile, in spite of myself.

I don't think I realised at the time, but that was a milestone moment. It was the first burst of energy I'd experienced since Saskia was admitted to hospital and it felt good. The eye-bags were paler than they had been, but my skin was dry and uncared for and would take more than a quick fix. I felt like a piece of driftwood dumped by a scummy tide. But this was a good day wasn't it? I was up and about to 'pull myself together' as Dad would say.

Poor Mum and Dad. It was especially hard for them. At least Tom and I could visit Saskia regularly, but for them it was nearly a two-hour journey from Cirencester when they could squeeze time out from the farm. Not easy with a herd of two hundred dairy cows. And when they got to us there was nothing they could do but sit and look at their only granddaughter as she slept.

Tom was home before me and was making himself a cup of tea in the kitchen.

'How was she Snooks?'

'No change but I put her pink frock on her and she looks very glammed-up. I think she would live up to her own exacting standards today.'

Tom kissed me. 'Would you like a cuppa?'

'Please. I'm coming with you this evening,' I announced. He dropped a teaspoon and grinned as if I'd peeled my clothes off and draped myself across the kitchen table. His eyes actually lit-up.

'Well done. Well done darling. I think we may both be turning a corner.' He kissed me again and I could swear he was damp-eyed. 'Got a bit of marking to do and then I'll be up for a shower.'

'We haven't got long.'

'I know. Half an hour - max. OK?'

Drinks weren't until six thirty which gave me time to armour myself for the onslaught of, *'How are you Lottie? Are you coping my dear?'*

People meant well but Saskia's coma was virgin territory for most people. And there was the drug issue too. I guessed Tom had had it tough trying to explain to the higher echelon of the college how his daughter was knifed and fell into a drug and alcohol fuelled coma. It must have been excruciating for him. Churchill's College was rife with drug-awareness programmes and susceptible lads whose parents spent a fortune to educate them. I worried if his job would be secure.

I was dreading the end of term and the parental onslaught. Tom had written to the parents of boys in our house to explain what had happened to Saskia. I didn't see the letter although I suspected it was sparse on detail. And of course, families would be concerned, and rightly so. One or two people had already been to see the Head to discuss the situation, and I knew I'd be worried if the tables were turned and it was my son living in our house. I would definitely expect my child to be kept safe at Churchill's and might even question the competency of a House Master whose daughter fell into such bad company.

Failure never sat well with Tom. He never discussed with me how colleagues accepted the news but then, we hadn't had many meaningful conversations at all. I had no idea how my oyster-shell husband was coping with his life and that alone piled further guilt on me. I hadn't been there for him for weeks and could only imagine he'd had embarrassing moments within the workplace. Perhaps I should have asked more questions.

*'Of course I can do this.'* I stared at my reflection in the mirror and took a long hard look at a face etched with grief; it was a face that had aged ten years in a few short weeks. The hair looked good though. I'd promised myself that the drinks party would be a turning point, and I was determined to grasp the moment and make solid strides towards getting my life back. Sadly, that wouldn't change the course of Saskia's coma, but it would make for a better atmosphere in the house and perhaps it would stop me drifting like a yacht with no rudder.

I wanted to find something stunning to wear to boost my confidence and also to please Tom. He'd found it hard to hide his irritation with my inability to get on with life. I'd always found his slightly anal view of things endearing, especially when I studied his ghastly mother and realised he was a miracle of manhood, all things considered. Despite being born to wealth and position and his mother's domineering ways, he had grown into the man I loved.

I knew Tom loved me. He showed it in little ways although he wasn't given to grand gestures. But I knew he'd be devastated if our marriage fell apart, even though neither of us had the tools to keep it together at that point. My mother told me not to worry. She thought our marriage was built on strong foundations and would, without doubt, survive. I hung onto every positive I could find.

Things weren't good in bed, either. But who could wonder about that? Our sex life had always been healthily frequent and modestly enthusiastic. But after the trauma, our time in bed meant nothing more than attempting to sleep and the endless task of shutting out the nightmare that defined our precious daughter. There was no touching, no cuddles, nothing between us that vaguely resembled affection, just the occasional robust effort at penetration from Tom and an acquiescence on my part. It never failed to amaze me how men can screw at the drop of a hat. They screw if they're angry, screw if they're on a high and screw if they need to forget. I've never been like that. A cuddle would have been a start. Just a touch that wasn't sexual might have moved things along a bit, but to expect full blown sex was like asking me to climb Mount Kilimanjaro without first burning calories at the gym and toning my body for the onslaught.

It was obvious I'd scored brownie points by joining Tom for the drinks party as he showered me with the enthusiasm of a first date. I chose white linen trousers and a turquoise cardigan over a grey vest which had a delicate sprinkling of diamanté around the neckline. I added chunky, white beads, grey low heels and a generous spray of L'eau de Issey.

Tom ushered me out of the house and treated me like a princess, albeit a fragile one who needed pampering. His arm around my shoulder felt reassuring in my current, cockeyed world. I knew I'd lost weight for the first time in years and despite my reluctance to look in mirrors, I'd sneaked an admiring glance at myself as we left. I noticed with satisfaction, the slim line hips which made the boobs look rather plumptious; an illusion for sure, but very nice.

Drinks with the dinosaur were not altogether unpleasant despite my embarrassment about our wayward daughter. Beaks and their wives were pussyfooting around us and only the brave actually referred to Saskia. I'd never been good with pitying looks and even less well disposed to academic males trying to show their sensitive side. So, I gravitated towards Heidi Brooker who was always good for a bit of schoolboy humour. She had a disarming way of getting to the nub of things without offending.

'Great to see you out, Honey.' She kissed me on both cheeks. 'You look fab darling and so sexy.

'Do I remember the connotations of sexy?' I asked her.

'Yeh yeh. You and Tom are the couple 'most likely.' You know, everyone thinks you have more than your share.'

I chuckled.

'I thought of you this morning. Hope you weren't listening to Radio 4.'

I hadn't been listening. I rarely bothered with TV or the radio. 'No. What did I miss?'

'Nothing you'd have wanted to hear. That sixth former from St. Katherine's in Oxford. The one who was missing? Her body's been found in the river and her father was being interviewed'.

'Poor thing. I'm not sure public dissection helps, to be honest.'

'Guess you always hope someone will throw a ray of light on evil, though.'

'Mm. And of course they might.'

'Are you sleeping better?

'Much better. Hurray for Amitriptyline.' Why would I tell anyone the truth about the nocturnal elf that hammered me with his doom and gloom antics?

'How are things with Tom?'

Trickier this one. 'We're managing. You know.'

'Bet you can't wait for the end of term.'

'I can't, but I think teaching helps Tom. It starves him of time to ponder. Unlike me. I'm due for a degree in pondering any time soon.'

Heidi smiled. 'Let's ponder another glass of bubbly, shall we?' She picked up two glasses of champagne and wouldn't take no for an answer when I told her I'd already had enough.

'After all you've been through. Get it down you Mrs Hanson!'

I noticed Tom was in deep conversation with the Head and another teacher whose name escaped me. Tom caught my eye and gave a brief wave. I knew he was keeping a close eye on me and who could blame him?

Heidi asked about Saskia and sympathised when I told her there had been no change. We talked about all the ramifications; nothing was off limits with Heidi. We talked about everything from Saskia imminently waking up to having her life-support switched off. Good old Heidi. She'd verbalised my greatest fear and it was the first time the words had been formed by someone else. It was welcome after dealing with the continuous loop of angst imbedded in my head.

Suddenly Tom was by my side. He smiled at Heidi and Anne Tilsley who had joined us. 'Great to see her out, isn't it girls?'

They both agreed it was.

'I'm afraid I'm going to steal her away, but coffee together could be on the agenda in the near future, couldn't it Snooks?'

I agreed it could. As I walked with him across the grass, he whispered in my ear. 'Needn't stay long,' he giggled like a naughty schoolboy. 'Just showing up for one glass of bubbly is enough.' He smiled at me and winked. 'Or two, or even three, if you like. It's high time you had a bit of fun, Darling.'

My low heels sank into the grass, and I took Tom's arm for support.

'Don't think the Head will even notice if we slip away, especially as the randy old goat can't take his eyes off the new science teacher.'

The nibbles looked delicious although I wasn't persuaded to nibble. I rather liked my new hips. Vintage Crug in Waterford flutes was held aloft on silver trays by ladies of a certain age who were dressed in black with frilly white pinafores. Years ago, when Tom and I first arrived at Churchill's my friends were amazed by their first brush with the establishment. *'God this place is stuck in the Middle Ages!'* was the cry. And probably it was. But I'd rarely needed to defend it in more recent years. I'd learnt to appreciate certain elements of life at Churchill's; the uniqueness, its provenance and the shear centuries of history melded into its stonework still tended to impress all but the most jaded. I suppose I particularly approved of its ability to remain unmoved and solid in a world that was rocking on its axis. Recently, the solid aspects of the old place held a degree of comfort, a feeling of belonging.

We made our way to talk to Ed Fenton as I wanted to ask if the baby had arrived. It hadn't. I noticed a small girl running around her mother's skirts and remembered the scurry of excitement when we knew Saskia was going to be ours. She was much the same age with similar energy.

It seemed it was only yesterday that we'd hugged and kissed a small girl into our lives. Preparation for Saskia's arrival had reached manic proportions and we were lucky to have a large house and garden in which to welcome her. The maintenance department was commandeered to paint her nursery before creating a child-proof outdoors which was fit for our princess. Money flowed into Harrods and staggered out in the form of pink and white toddler paraphernalia delivered by polite men in green vans. Nothing was too good for our new arrival.

'I expect the end of term will be a blessing Lottie.'

I jumped as the deputy head smiled down on me with sympathetic eyes. At six foot six he tended to look down on most people, but he made me feel petite and vulnerable.

'I think so John. But to be honest, one day is much like another, at the moment. The boys are definitely a distraction for Tom.'

'Any change? Any good news about Saskia?'

'Not yet but we're hopeful. Thanks for....'

Tom interrupted. 'I've just had a call from the house Darling. Sorry John, I have to deprive you of my lovely wife. We need to get back.'

'My loss, Old Boy. Good to see you out and about again Lottie. Don't forget, everyone is here for you. Just ask. You've been missed.'

'Thanks John. You're very kind.'

Tom ushered me away and then started to giggle.

'That worked.'

'What? What worked?'

'There's been no phone call Snooks. Just used the idea as an excuse to extract ourselves. Thought you'd be pleased.'

'I am.' I smiled at him. It was unusual for Tom to play hooky around school duties, and I felt well rewarded for the effort I'd made with my appearance.

We walked home and took the shortcut around the gym and across the tennis courts. I could see the river on its never-ending journey through the willow trees and realised it had been weeks since I'd walked that way. I decided to walk somewhere the next day, even if it was only to the shops.

The house was quiet, as it should have been when we arrived back. The boys were doing their evening prep. I caught a look from Tom that told me he had one thing on his mind and, happily, I found I could cope. No, I could do better than cope; I was looking forward to it.

Tom found the junior master who'd been house-sitting and told him we were back. The bespectacled young man scurried off, no doubt to do a pile of marking or lesson preparation for the next day. I offered Tom my services to ensure all was well with the boys.

'Shall I check on the sixth form common room for you?'

'Thanks. They always prefer it when you stick your head round the door. I'm not flavour of the month at the moment. Not since I vetoed the end of term party.'

'I'll do it then. I'll see if Lovett's back after tea with the grandparents, too.'

'You're an angel. Just check that Aspinall is around. He has a tendency to skip off to town on Thursday evenings. Some girl waits by Marks and Spencer for him.'

'Spoil sport! I'll see if he's in. Shall I cook? Chef's left us a salad but I can probably do better than that.'

'Umm. That would be great.'

Tom always had a good appetite after sex, so I raided the freezer for some fish and a chocolate pudding that required a puddle of chocolate sauce. Tom would think it was his birthday.

My husband was full of high spirits. He locked our apartment door and put the 'see matron' sign up. I was a bit giggly having eaten very little and not bothered with alcohol for weeks. Unsurprisingly, champagne had gone straight to my head.

Tom scooped me up like a bride on her wedding day and plonked me playfully on our huge bed. Enid had changed the sheets that morning which always enticed my husband.

I could see both of us in the dressing-table mirror and a slight, feel-good-factor lifted the burden on my heart. Sex was surely a step forward, even if we knew we had the champagne to thank for our enthusiasm.

Tom kissed me and I kissed him back. He stroked my cheek and lifted my hand to his lips. 'You're still as beautiful as the day I married you. I'm going to take better care of you.' I wanted to make a smart-ass remark about wrinkles and eye-bags, but I bit it back and kissed him with such enthusiasm that we tumbled like kittens across the fresh linen.

He slid the cardigan off my shoulders and kissed the nape of my neck. Tingles shot across my shoulders as his fingers eased one strap of my vest down my arm. I helped with the other. Soon he reached for my breast and took a nipple in his mouth. I felt a pulse that hadn't been encouraged to beat for weeks.

Tom shed his clothes like a teenager and left them in a pile on the floor. I constantly told the boys to refrain from doing that, but this was my fully-grown, sexy husband and he wanted to fuck me. And I was grateful. Grateful that he still wanted the miserable specimen I'd become, and I was grateful that maybe, just maybe, I could get a life back, regardless of the trauma with Saskia. He eased my trousers over my new, slim line hips and his fingers searched around the lace on my thong.

***

**Tracey**

I was worried about my boy and went to see him again. I rang the prison and said it was urgent because I was scared for him. 'Cos he was on remand he could have visitors four times a week so they agreed I could pick up a visiting order at Reception when I arrived.

The number fifteen bus was late, so I nearly missed me connection and it was bloody bucketing down, again. I 'spose I was lucky I got there at all. And there was one hell of a queue to get in and the dogs were sniffing about again. As if I'd be daft enough to bring drugs in. They made a young girl with a baby take off the kid's nappy to check for something. I thought, OMG, surely they don't smuggle drugs in on their kids?

There were lockers we had to use. Everything had to go in, including handbags and coats. Some bloke in the queue told me it was done so that we couldn't pass anything across to prisoners. A woman was patting down the female visitors and I wished she'd hurry up. I couldn't wait to see my Alfie.

'So how are things then? A simple enough question but it opened the floodgates. He seemed more depressed than the last time I saw him.

'All I can hear is the clanging of keys; metal grating in locks.'

I noticed he was awfully pale. It didn't help that they dressed them all in dishwater grey.

'It's just like on the tele in here and...to be honest Mum, I'm scared shitless.'

If my Alfie was scared then I knew it was bad.

'The trouble is,' he said, 'I don't know how long I'll be here.'

It was hard for both of us to get our heads around things. We both knew he could get anything up to ten years.

'But I never fucking did it, Mum. I love her.'

I looked at him and searched those deep brown eyes. It sounded like the truth to me, but it would to his mother, wouldn't it?

'I'm gonna plead not guilty. Course I am. I never done it Mum.'

It broke my heart to see him. I kept imagining that little kid with wings on his heels. Such high hopes I had for him. But now he was angry. I could see it in his eyes, and I could understand it, too.

'I saw you in my court hearing, but you never smiled at me once.'

He sounded like a little boy who needed to lay blame.

'I was too damn scared to smile. And I was hoping they'd grant you bail. I was holding my breath while we waited to know. Snotty cow of a judge, wasn't she? When she remanded you, I was well pissed off,' I told him.

'You were pissed-off? I was shitting meself.'

I looked at his little face and wanted to put my hand over his, but I dared not touch him.

'Little people like us never get a break, do we?' I noticed the Visit's Hall had filled to bursting and the noise level was somewhere near a Blur concert. Alfie was biting his nails.

'You had a look on yer face like you used to give me when I was a kid. When I lied and you sussed me? Remember? Well, you've got it wrong this time Mum 'cos I never done it.'

'I never thought....' I tried to spit the words out.... 'I was just wondering why your prints were on the knife.'

'Ha. Thought so. You think I did it. I knew it.'

I could feel tears trying to have their way on my face and I looked out of the window. 'Alfie,' I tried again, 'you need to know I'm right here fer you. No matter what happens. OK?' He didn't answer and I was desperate for him to know I'd got his back.

After a while he was ready to spill again. It was like he was battery-charged. 'Thing is Mum, now they've found my fingerprints on the knife, no matter how many times I tell 'em what happened, nobody believes I tried to save Saskia. I grabbed the knife to stop that wanker hurting her.' I could see tears in his eyes. 'And next thing I know, she's bleeding like a stuck pig. My beautiful girl was bleeding in front of me eyes. I was so scared Mum. I had no idea what to do.'

I was imagining the scene. It must have been mayhem.

'She kept screaming at me to leave her alone. She screamed like a demented animal. I wanted to stay with her, but she was making so much noise... I ran. I ran so fast my brain couldn't keep up with me. I wanted to find you 'cos I knew you'd tell me what to do.' He was getting agitated just remembering it all.

'Keep it down over there.' A big bloke in uniform eyeballed us.

'Wanker.' Alfie flashed a look I'd seen a million times before. At least there was a bit of spark left in him.

'Why it never crossed my mind to dial 999 I'll never know. I never seem to latch on to doing the right thing in a crisis, do I? And 'cos I didn't do the right thing, Saskia might die. I'm stuck in here and I want to see her.'

I watched the officers as they scanned the room. They eyeballed us like we were all criminals. There was a woman doing teas and I wandered over to get a couple. They had to be free 'cos they'd taken everybody's handbag away.

'There's nothing to do here,' Alfie said as he slurped his tea and made a face. 'Shit, ain't it?' He looked at his plastic cup. 'Why the hell can't they make a simple cup of tea?' He slurped it anyway. 'There's nothing to do here Mum. It's driving me nuts.'

He started to tell me about life on the wing, like he needed to get things off his chest. He chuckled when he told me about a screw working her way along the landing that morning. He said you could hear her yelling two cells down. 'Get out Osborne and wash your filthy self,' she shouted at the top of her voice.

'You can hear everything in here. And she's right. Osborne stinks. My door flew open like she wanted to take it off the hinges. 'Shower, Collins.' And then I heard myself say 'Yes Miss.' Can you imagine me saying that?'

I couldn't. It made me chuckle as I watched a dark cloud cross the window. It looked like it might rain again, soon.

He told me, 'I picked up my wash stuff and followed her along the landing like a little kid.'

That made me laugh too, despite the grimness of it all. 'You ain't never toed the line since you were a nipper, so I don't think you'll be starting in here,' I reminded him. But he seemed determined to tell me the tale of going to the showers. I told him to keep his voice down a bit.

'Officer Pershore is butch and meaty,' he said. Blokes in here love her but she ain't nothing like any sexual fantasy I've ever had.

It felt like too much information from my grown-up son but I was there for whatever he needed to get off his chest. I looked at the snooty cow on point duty to see if she'd heard him, but she was too busy talking to notice us. I could sense Alfie wanted to tell me more. It was like he'd had nobody to talk to for days.

'According to Crunchy, it's only a matter of time before I start fancying her, too. They all want to give her one.'

I couldn't help smiling even if it was a bit near the mark. At least he'd cheered up a bit.

'Look at the tits,' Crunchy said. 'Forget the ass and concentrate on the tits man.'

'Ssh! You'll get locked down if you keep on.'

I asked him what his cell was like. Was the bed comfy? Anything to change the subject.

'It's OK. I'm sharing with a miserable sod who tried to get the night safe out of Barclays Bank. Idiot.'

Then he told me how he had to give all his possessions the quick once over every time they took him out of his cell. 'The thieving bastards in here'll nick anything. And the screws spin your cell whenever they want. But I'm not daft. I've hidden my slicer somewhere they'll never find it. You have to get savvy pretty quick in here otherwise they find all yer illegals.'

'What slicer!'

'Ssh Mum, keep yer voice down.'

He looked around like a ferret to see if I'd attracted attention then leaned over the table as far as he dared. 'You have to learn to look after yerself. It's bloody dangerous in here. And it cost too much to get hold of a slicer to let the screws find it.'

It all sounded like something off the tele to me, but the words were falling from his mouth like vomit. I wanted to ask what he planned to do with the slicer, but the words got stuck in my throat. There was no shutting my Alfie up.

'You have to blag stuff off blokes and that costs money. Or a splif, if you've got one. You can get most things done for a splif. Now I've got something to hide, I have to be bloody careful.'

I thought the silly sod was going to get caught doing something he shouldn't and then they'd eat him for breakfast. I knew he was heading for trouble.

'Now you listen to me,' I told him. 'Don't you think it's bad enough just being in here, without making matters ten times worse? Keep yer bloody head down, you pillock.' I could feel my temper rising but I dared not make a fuss. 'I better go before I say something I'll regret. You'll keep your nose clean, if you know what's good for you.'

And I missed the bloody bus home.

***

*Mummy...the horrible man got off me and I didn't see him again... Alfie wanted to take the knife out of my stomach, and he tried to stop the bleeding with his shirt. I remember screaming. I wanted you to come and find me, but you didn't... Alfie said I should go with him, and he'd fix me up, but I was so scared... I could feel how much blood was on my dress and I was afraid I was going to die, Mummy. I still felt dizzy... probably because I'd drunk so much vodka.*

## Lottie

People often remarked that Tom and I proved the rule that opposites attract, and I suppose we did in many ways. We wove a path around all our differences and created a brand-new tapestry filled with a life we both loved.

We'd met when we were undergraduates; both of us were gung-ho, *'take a bite out of life'* students and we gelled like limpets on a rock. I never looked at anyone after I met Tom Hanson.

Our backgrounds held few similarities. My husband had a silver spoon well and truly thrust into his delicious, sensuous mouth from the day he was born while I was born onto a working farm with loving, but frugal, parents. While Tom had free access to the world of gap-year travel, long before it became the norm, I was earning money on my paper-round.

Tom deferred his place at Oxford not once, but twice. It's amazing what can be done when influence comes as standard down the family bloodline. I, on the other hand, grabbed my offer and went up before someone else took my place. So, when Tom eventually tipped up at Oxford he had an enviable air of 'a *man about town*'. Sports cars, suntans gained on the ski slopes and girls who hung on his every word were fodder for a rather shy and unassuming Tom.

I must say, money never spoilt Tom. He was a quiet, thoughtful man, especially wary of the giggly, blue-stocking-brigade. I remember he always looked put out by too much attention. Silly girls made him frown and over-indulgence in any form still makes him uncomfortable.

While Tom was working through the more suitable girls at university and failing to notice me, I didn't let the grass grow under my size seven and a half feet. I was tall, gangly as a young giraffe and feisty with it.

I worked hard but embraced student life to the full and I had a ball, literally, attending every party, function and college society going. Life at Oxford had limitations for me, mainly financial ones, but I managed to wring every last cent from my grant. When the money dried up there was always a willing suitor to step into the breach.

After life in Parochial Cirencester, I couldn't believe the buzz of Oxford. As the daughter of third generation, working farmers I had a firm handle on life without perks. Early morning milking for pocket money, helping with the harvest for the fun of it and delivering a stillborn calf with the knowledge of a vet, all became second nature to me by the time I was thirteen.

'Don't know where the brains come from,' Dad frequently uttered. His pride in my achievements at the local grammar school knew no bounds and he slaved night and day to get the money required for me to live the life of an Oxford undergraduate.

'Just drop your mother a line now and then,' he asked. And I did. Religiously, every week I dropped a postcard or letter into the box in the college wall and never failed to tell them what a great life they'd given me.

As the second son of titled parents, Tom had always known his elder brother would inherit both title and fortune. And he never cared. But when their plans were shattered and their father died of cancer while Tom and his brother were both in their teens, things changed at a pace. His elder brother had to step up to the plate, long before he was ready. He'd never married although his mother begged him to 'make a smart choice of wife'. Only Tom knew his brother was gay.

The responsibility of the estate barely touched Tom's life as he grew up. He'd been gifted a free choice of career and always thought he was the lucky one. He had no desire to be molded into the Squire of the estate by an over-bearing, widowed mother. It was therefore an unbelievable shock when his brother also died, shortly after we were married.

When reality sank in and the initial grieving was sated, we discovered Tom's mother, or as I liked to call her, 'the grand dame,' had expectation that Tom would abandon his chosen career and return home to live on the estate. Tom and I agreed that when his mother died we would reconsider, but she was as strong as an ox, and we could face that dilemma when it occurred. Meanwhile, his mother bullied and harassed him to such a degree that we rarely visited her. I considered it to be her loss that she never became close to Saskia, although I don't believe Saskia suffered by the omission.

At the age of four Saskia attended a local prep school just a mile down the road from where we lived. Money and privilege fluttered down on the pampered children like confetti. My Dad said she should have gone to the local primary school, if only to keep her grounded, but we were more than happy with our choice.

We debated where Saskia should be schooled when she was eleven. 'If she doesn't get away this year', Tom said, 'we'll have raging hormones in the house which will keep us awake at night. I can't cope with a teenager creeping around dorms in the early hours of the morning. Especially when she's mine. She'll be seeking to fulfil lustful urges she's too damned young to be feeling.' Prophetic, I called it years later.

We both recognised the need to give our daughter a more balanced view of life which inevitably meant an all-girl's school. She'd been deluged by boys since she was two. So, at the age of eleven, and after much soul searching, we sent Saskia to a boarding school in Cheltenham. Having her grandparents in nearby Cirencester went some way to calming our anxieties as Saskia could have weekend exeats on the farm and enjoy a rather more grown-up relationship with Granny and Pops. I was keen for her to have some of the solid grounding my parents had given me. I thought it would do my daughter good to see how the other half lived.

Mum and Dad were thrilled when we chose Cheltenham for Saskia's senior education. 'I'll teach her to milk the cows on weekends,' Dad announced. 'You'll do no such thing,' Mum told him. 'She'll be a lady when she grows up. Tom has a title, even though he don't use it. Remember that.'

It took Saskia some time to catch up with her peer group's interest in boys. *What's so special about boys?* But eventually she began to view them in a more favourable light. We picked up the odd reference to a Dominic, who'd taken her to the cinema and a Liam she met at a social school. All harmless, we were sure. Looking back, I realise how naïve I was.

Saskia promised us she had thrown herself into work, however, according to her letters and telephone calls she also enjoyed hockey, lacrosse and tennis and an introduction to makeup, fashion and flirting. I didn't always show Tom what she wrote as he would have had words with her. If we'd had the large family we longed for, maybe he wouldn't have been so obsessive about our only daughter.

About six months before Saskia was due to make her A level choices, to everyone's surprise Churchill's decided to admit girls into the sixth form. This had been a major discussion point for years, especially by the dyed-in-the-wool crustaceans who never wanted change to their revered Churchill's College. But it gave us much to consider, not least the financial implications of moving Saskia back home. We would be entitled to considerably discounted school fees at Churchill's.

When we consulted Saskia about the new possibility, she told us she could see advantages in both options. Eventually, it was agreed that she would take her A levels at Churchill's, and we duly gave notice to Cheltenham. We looked back on that decision later and realised what a massive mistake it had been, but we could never have foreseen quite how catastrophic.

As she entered her first term of sixth form at Churchill's it was noted that Saskia had blossomed into a confident young woman with no sign of the previous 'chummy' relationships with the boys in the house. Instead, she developed a competitive aloofness which calmed most of our fears. We told each other it looked highly unlikely Saskia would show any inclination towards the opposite sex for at least another year. How very wrong we were to bumble along our merry way, rejoicing in the fact that our darling daughter was home.

Mum and Dad loved to visit us, preferably during holiday times. Dad was always like a cat on hot bricks around the boys and they had a tendency to call him 'Sir 'which was one step too far for a dairy farmer. Mum found it easier. 'They're just normal little boys underneath the plummy accent and the posh clothes', she often observed. And she was right.

Over the years we'd sorted a myriad of problems for the boys; things that even money and breeding couldn't combat. Heartache, divorce, deaths, abandonment and police cautions all came our way. But when some of the boys came back to see us as confident young men who had made their way in the world, we were as proud as any parent. They even brought their new wives and babies on occasion, and I loved to see them all. Tom could be more aloof, but that's just Tom. I suppose Churchill's ways were more deeply ingrained in him than they were in me.

One morning, I was drinking coffee in the kitchen, probably dreaming about our daughter coming home when Tom appeared in the doorway. 'Snooks. Ah, there you are?'

I glanced up from the kitchen table where I was looking up the family chocolate cake recipe. I was only looking. I hadn't any intention to make it.

'Hi. Didn't expect to see you. Is everything all right?'

He looked at me for a full ten seconds; it was enough time for my stomach to flip and my mouth to dry-out. 'Oh God! What? What's happened?' I scraped the chair across the stone floor and went to him.

'Nothing. Nothing that I know of, anyway. Mark Erdington wants to see us at eleven. I've got cover for my lessons.' He put a reassuring arm across my shoulder. Very Tom-like.

'Did it sound like bad news?'

'It didn't sound like anything Snooks. It was his secretary who called. Let's stay calm.

The transient joys of a few nights earlier seemed light years away and fear stalked a familiar pathway. But Tom played devil's advocate.

'You never know, it could be good news. Obviously, we'd have been called to the ward if Saskia had woken. But they could still have something positive to tell us.'

I didn't have a good feeling about it. I racked my brains to remember if any test results were due that day, but I couldn't think of anything.

'Have you had breakfast? You should eat something, Snooks.'

'You'd hate to stare at a puddle of vomit.'

'OK. You know best.'

I knew Tom had made himself a bowl of porridge before school, as witnessed by the aftermath of milk and brown sugar floating in congealed lumpiness in the sink. I've always had an aversion to porridge.

'How about eating some dry toast? Something to line the old stomach?'

Darling Tom. Sometimes it was like living with my mother.

'I can't give food a passing thought. What if... they want to switch off her life support?' I blurted as warm, salty tears ran down my face.

'Hey. None of that. We're looking at the positives, remember?'

I didn't remember that conversation, but I did remember every bloody thing I'd read about comas, and I knew the day could arrive when there was no point in keeping the patient alive. That was fine for others, but not for Saskia. I'd fight with my bare hands if I had to, I'd do anything to keep my daughter alive. 'I'll have another coffee,' I said to appease Tom. 'Shall I make enough for you too?' He was deep in his own thoughts. It was easy to forget how tough it was for him as he always appeared so in control of his emotions. 'Would you like coffee? I repeated.'

 'Good idea.' He smiled at me with his autumn-leaves eyes and slid his specs up his nose while he delved into the cupboard for coffee mugs. 'The traffic on the bypass shouldn't be too bad at this time of day.'

I really didn't want the coffee, but I gulped it down to please him. Coffee and breakfast seemed so mundane that morning. I asked myself, what if it was the day we had to say goodbye to her? Forever. It was more than I could bear and I headed for the bedroom to compose myself. Poor Tom hated to see me upset and he'd had rather a lot of upset to contend with over the past few weeks.

We set off in Tom's car; I knew he didn't trust me to drive. I turned off the radio which was tuned to Classic FM. Every sound grated and annoyed. And then I obsessed over the radio; first it's on and then, at the flick of a switch, it's off. Just like a life-support machine.

I tried to find something new to look at outside the car window on a journey we'd made a hundred times before. Make that a thousand if you included trips to the hospital with boys from the House. I noticed a woman grab a small boy before he ran into the road. Hold on to him, I thought. Never take your eyes off him unless you want a tragedy in your family. I could feel hot tears forming in readiness to cascade down my blotchy face. I needed to get a hold of my emotions as I couldn't blub in Mark Erdington's office. Tom would be mortified. But actually, did I give a shit?

I mused about my daughter who, by the age of seven was at best, precocious and often downright demanding. I suppose we spoilt her as is the tendency of parents who wait for the gift of a child to come their way. And as she grew, we and the boys in our house loved her more. Saskia could spit venom as often as she'd grace you with her smile, but everyone forgave her the tantrums.

Saskia was always the tallest and the prettiest in her class. Well, I thought so. Although her genes were not ours, she seemed to take after Tom with an innate slimness and height that promised to last, given a chance. My autumnal colours were reflected in her face and russet hair and she had my large feet. What were the chances of those similarities in an adopted child?

By the time we reached the hospital and found a parking space, my mind was made up. It was going to be a life-support issue that was up for discussion and my adrenaline was pumping. As we made our way to the fourth floor it felt odd that we weren't visiting Saskia on the ward.

Mark's office was in one of the signature gloss-painted corridors and his secretary was busy in the room next door to his. She smiled. 'Mr and Mrs Hanson? Mr Erdington will only be five minutes. Can I get you coffee?' We declined her offer. Instead, we sat in a busy corridor observing the comings and goings of normal people. Those without a daughter lying in a coma. *I used to be like you*, I thought. *I had no worries. I had the perfect life.*

Mark appeared after a ten-minute wait, and we were seated in front of his desk with the door firmly closed. I've never been good behind closed doors and my pulse thumped and sickness threatened. I gave myself a stern talking to and turned to Mark. 'This has given us both a scare. Being called in like this.'

'I know. I'm sorry Lottie. What I have to say has only come to light this morning.'

A sound escaped and I didn't know if it came from me or Tom. I felt his hand on mine and tried to gather comfort from the gentle squeeze.

'First I have to apologise.'

*Shit, forget the apology and get on with it. Please.*

'We missed something that should have been spotted earlier. There's no easy way to tell you but... Saskia is pregnant.'

I could hear a car alarm in the distance; it was probably in the hospital car park and belonged to someone who needed a simple x-ray. Or it belonged to a normal person, someone who hadn't had their world turned upside down for the second time in the last few weeks. I decided to wait until someone turned it off. I kept my eyes on the window although there was only a grey stone wall staring back. But it was firm and unmoving. It had no frills or complications. It was just a grey wall.

'Lottie.' It was Tom grabbing my attention and I appeared to have missed something.'

'Yes. Yes, I heard. Saskia's pregnant.' The car alarm was still jarring on my thought process.

'Are you alright darling?'

I knew blood had drained from my face and I didn't trust my legs to function. There was no escape. 'Of course,' I said. 'What's another crisis? What else can life throw at us?'

And then I was taken to another place, and I didn't feel it coming. Not one signal emerged to warn me before I curled my body onto my knees and sobs gushed from somewhere deep, low and painful. Tom wrapped his arms around me, but they didn't make me feel safe. I thought I would never feel safe again. How much worse could things get? Did he rape her, or did she lie on her back and open her legs to him? I tortured myself with hideous flashes of rampant teenage sex and fought the urge to vomit on Mark's floor. I noticed it wasn't carpeted so...that was all right then. A mop and bucket with some strong disinfectant would do the job. Still, no one switched off that bloody car alarm.

I grasped the pristine white handkerchief Tom found in his pocket, curtesy of reliable Enid, and tried to mop myself up. But the tears wouldn't stop. It was as if all the weeks of coping and putting on a brave face had crumbled into this moment.

'Tom, I'll give you a few minutes alone. I'm only next door.'

'Thanks. She'll be OK when I talk to her. I'll sort it out.'

'Of course.' Mark left us alone.

I suppose knowing that Tom would 'sort it out' should have been a crumb of comfort but it made me mad. I felt mad as hell with Tom, for no reason I could explain.

'Sort it out!' My voice was louder than he liked. 'This isn't one of your boys who's failed an A level. How can you 'sort it out'? You're not bloody Merlin.'

'Lottie, please. Not here. We need to go home and talk about this.'

'It feels a bit late for talking. Don't you think?'

'I'll go next door and tell Mark we're going home. I think we'll need to see him again in a couple of days.'

'OK'. I'm still crying although the deep sobs have subsided.'

'That's the ticket Snooks. Why don't you pop into the ladies while I see Mark?'

'Um...I'll see you along the corridor then.'

I headed to the loo, more to look in the mirror than anything else but then I wished I hadn't. I probably wouldn't bump into anyone I knew, so who cared that I looked like a demented hamster? I wanted to see my daughter.

***

## Tracey

Old Dickie's came to see if I was alright. 'Course I wasn't. Me lad was inside. 'He says he don't want to see ya,' I told him with a smirk, after he'd settled his ass on my sofa. 'So don't you go near him.'

'I know,' he said. 'Some tart at the prison refused me a visiting order when I rang.

'Why would he? Want to see you? When he knows what you've done to....'

'Yeh, yeh. Always moaning you are. I wouldn't mind, but he needs putting in the know – about all the things he'll need inside'.

'Like what? I can take them in.'

'Shan't fuckin bother to tell you. Got money, has he?'

'Too much money. That's half his problem. Too much bloody money,' I told him.

'Well, he shouldn't get in trouble then. Not if he's got money.'

'What sort of trouble?' I searched Dickie's eyes for signs that he was lying. I had plenty of experience of that. After years of playing off my need for him to babysit Lily against the vile things he'd made me do, I always came out worse.

'Don't know if I should tell you really. I only know 'cos me neighbour's nephew, Greggo Hewitt, is on the same wing.'

'And?'

'You sure you want to know? Don't whinge at me if you don't like it.'

'Course I want to know. What'd you take me for? A wuss?'

Dickie took time to blow his nose. He snuffled and snorted like a hedgehog after milk. 'Ok. You asked for it. There's a nonce on the wing who's taken a fancy to your Alfie. Big bugger. Says he's got a passion for black haired youngsters. Likes your Alfie's skin, he said.'

'What!' I felt the blood drain from my face. 'You gotta be kidding me. Alfie ain't no nonce.'

'Never said he was. This bloke just takes what he fancies. They call him the "*shower- shagger*" 'cos.... Well, I'm sure you can fill in the details.'

I had to sit down. Alfie was a lot of things, but he wouldn't go near a nonce. He'd had more women than I'd had hot dinners.

'Then of course, there's the drug-gangs. Got any drug debt, your Alfie?

How the hell did I know?

'I can help fix it all for him, you know.' I recognised that whining voice. And his eyes told me there was a catch.

'Oh yeh. And how can *you* keep my Alfie safe? Going in for a stretch, are yer?'

'Not me. Greggo Hewitt's already in there, like I told you, and he's prepared to make a little deal with you.'

'Why me? What's he want with me?' I knew things were taking a wrong turn. I stared out the window at a couple of lads playing footie and remembered when me and Alfie did that. I went to the sideboard and brought out a bottle of sherry left over from Christmas. I poured myself a full tumbler and didn't offer any to Dickie.

'There's lots of help you can get for the boy. Especially if you're prepared to do a favour in return. See what I mean?' he wheedled.

I kinda did but I didn't like the sound of it. Dickie went to put the kettle on, just like the old days. Thought he still owned me. But I was older, stronger and I could cope with Dickie and his dirty little ways. Especially with some sweet sherry inside me.

'There you go me little Pigeon Pie.' He put two mugs of tea on the table. It was like he's never noticed I was drinking sherry. He had a sort of soft look about him, too. He looked needy. Well, I wasn't going near his 'old man'- that much was certain. Those days were gone. Thought it would have shriveled up to nothing, anyway.

'Sugar, Pigeon?''

'I don't take sugar, you forgetful old fart. Spit it out then. Might as well cut to the chase.'

'Not so hasty. You always were hasty. Sometimes you've gotta just mull things over a bit. See how it fits.'

'So how exactly does it *fit*?'

'I'm just thinking how this could work. Best fer everybody. You know?'

I hadn't got a clue what he was talking about. 'Best fer you, you mean?'

'I could be hurt by that remark if I didn't know you. Luckily, I know yer don't mean it. Always spouting yer mouth off, ain't you?'

I couldn't argue with that. Mum always said I'd got a mouth like a barn door. She could talk. 'I still don't get it. Talk clear, will you?'

Dickie took a slurp of tea while I glugged back another mouthful of sherry. I was sick to my stomach worrying about what was coming. He added another spoonful of sugar to his mug and made me wait.

'OK. .......OK.......It's like this. Greggo said he's got a bit of business what's going to waste. He needs help on the outside, you know?'

I didn't know, but I had a pretty good idea it would involve sex.

'He said he'll keep an eye on Alfie for you, he'll see no nonce gets him up the... well you know what I mean. Get me drift? But it depends if you can do a bit of business for him.

OMG. I was already imagining Alfie being hurt. He'd put up a fight for sure, but they'd loved that, didn't they? Nonces. 'What sort of business?' I already knew I was done for. How could I let Alfie get hurt in prison?'

'Well here's the thing. Ever heard of DODO?'

I shook my head. I wasn't letting on to him.

Dickie chuckled. 'This is stuff...' He took time to blow his nose like a bleeding fanfare, 'made in back-room kitchens, it is. They say it's real strong stuff. It's the best currency there is in jail at the moment. Prisons are rife with it, right across the country.

'I aint peddling drugs. I've got my Lily to think about. Who'd look after her if I was inside? Me bleeding mother? I don't think so.'

'No... yer not getting it.'

'That's 'cos you ain't telling it straight.'

'OK. This is the thing. DODO is passing round in prison like a whore's panties.' He's looking at me like I'm daft. Like I don't know nothing about drugs.

'Yeh. And?

'But it's got to be paid for, of course. Know how they do that?

I hadn't got a clue but had an idea I soon would.

'They take the money off the little woman indoors. Her left at home with the kids. That's how.'

In about half an hour, after two cups of tea and much wheedling by Dickie, I had the lot. The men buy the DODO that's been smuggled into prison and the wives pay their bills. The deal on the table was that I set up a credit round, collecting money each week from the families of the local prisoners.

Dickie told me sometimes I'd have to travel quite a few miles and they'd give me a car with my own driver. He also said they liked to have a woman call for the money 'cos it didn't look as suspicious as a bloke. The old bastard even suggested I take Lily with me. Like hell I would. He reckoned the Old Bill got wise to the game after a time, so I'd have to go careful.

I said I'd think about it.

'Don't think too long 'cos you never know who might be stretching Alfie a bit.'

Shit. I wondered if he meant what I thought he meant.

***

*Mummy...I made Alfie leave me. I yelled at him to leave me alone. I was so scared. There was so much blood I... and when he left me, I realised I should have gone with him... I started to feel really cold and sleepy and I didn't care anymore. I wanted to float away... It felt as if I was in a huge balloon floating in the clouds. ... I....*

**Lottie**

I could tell the first real fall-out in our marriage was on the horizon. After our meeting with Mark Erdington and the devastating blow that Saskia was pregnant, the journey home was no more than a blur. But somehow we arrived at the house and Tom went to have a quiet word with Enid. I think he told her our news and suggested she went home early. I never agreed with his habit of treating her as a member of the family; I would have preferred no one knew until we'd had time to discuss it, but that was typical Tom.

I inhabited a space in the kitchen, but it could just as well have been on the moon. It was the same kitchen where Tom had made coffee that morning and I sat in my usual chair. The scrubbed wooden table had familiar veins, lines and ink splodges that marked decades of other people's family crisis', but today it would need a knife to inflict a gouge that was deep enough to mark our family's distress. I thought the news was more than my wrung-out body could take.

The view of the garden was unchanged. How was that possible? It was so calm and beautiful out there, but it made me want to scream; I wanted to pull up the bulbs and slash the rose bushes to the ground. I wanted to be Saskia and disappear into a deep sleep. I'd rather have been anyone but me at that moment.

Tom was holding a bottle of gin. He didn't ask but poured two large ones. Even in our merciless state of despair, he managed to find ice and lemon. God forbid anyone at Churchill's drank gin without ice and lemon. He sat opposite me and watched as I gulped the top third of the content from my glass, all in one desperate slurp. I felt Tom was willing me to say something, but I couldn't.

'Termination is the only route Snooks. The sooner we get it done the better.' His look was one I'd learned to read over the years; a small frown rippled across his forehead, followed by a purse of his lips which made them momentarily lopsided. He hated it when I told him his mother had the same facial expression when she felt obliged to air-kiss me. I knew the expression to be one of determination and one that seldom lost an argument.

My silence worried me - would Tom take my silence as an agreement? I stared out of the window some more. I visualised a sperm, valiantly swimming against the tide; I saw a small life on a survival mission. I chose to ignore any ownership of the sperm or indeed the egg it was about to fertilise. And I didn't even equate it with my beautiful daughter. But I remembered how we longed for it to happen for us; we ached for a sperm to find the right egg, just one little egg didn't seem so much to ask, to have the child we longed for. But it never happened. How cruel Mother Nature can be, and she'd certainly got a sense of humour. I couldn't answer Tom because I was numb. I knew exactly what he'd said but I was frozen by the thought that our grandchild could be scraped down a sluice.

'Snooks? 'Tom puts his hand across the table and brushed my arm. 'You must know I'm right. What other option is there?'

I could see a new life in my arms; a bundle in white cloth that deserved the chance to live. What if Saskia's birthmother had scraped her away? We would never have had the delight of being her parent. And I wondered about our daughter. What was best for her? What would she want when she woke up? I decided this conversation could wait for another day, so I made an excuse and left my husband sitting in contemplation at the kitchen table.

I couldn't ignore the irony of it all. We'd offered Saskia a new bedroom to welcome her home from Cheltenham.

'Why not take over the yellow guest room?' Tom suggested during her last term at Cheltenham. 'An en-suite and enough space for a sofa and a desk should make it feel rather grownup, don't you think?'

Our beautiful daughter bubbled with excitement at the thought of her new room. The next few weeks saw a flurry of college painters challenged to find the perfect shade of pink to satisfy an exacting sixteen-year-old. She chose the same colour for the walls as the lilies near the rose trellis. I remembered the wind had got them that year. New furniture appeared, a four-poster bed complete with drapes in the sheerest muslin and a cream carpet which I assured her would show every mark, but it was approved anyhow.

Saskia planned to access medical school after a gap year spent in some warm and exotic location, far from parental guidance. Her main A level subjects were the Sciences, and it was therefore, just by chance, that she visited the college art-rooms with her father one Saturday afternoon.

'Give your old father a treat. Come with me to see the Art Exhibition in the Punchard Rooms,' he teased her.

'Sure. Could you wait for me to change?' Saskia bounded off like a new-born filly to beautify herself.

How she looked had become of vital importance to her.

'You come too Snooks. You haven't seen any of the boy's art this year.'

'I've promised to visit Belle. The new granddaughter is staying for the weekend and admiration is obligatory. Maybe next weekend.'

Tom waited for our daughter to appear in whatever dress was considered de-rigour to visit an art gallery.

'I must say, it's a treat to have half an hour or so of my daughter's undivided attention,' he said.

'Daddy! I'm always around these days.'

'Hmm... It seems I always have to share you these days. I suppose when you have a beautiful daughter, everyone wants a piece of Saskia, don't they?'

'Daddy!' Saskia blushed.

I watched them saunter through the school grounds and they left me awash with a warm feeling which reflected our life since Saskia came along. Fourteen years of happiness was an immeasurable joy. As father and daughter walked arm in arm, I remember thinking how lovely it was to see them so close.

As I changed for my coffee stop at Belle's, I imagined them entering the sanctified portal of student art, breathing in pungent turpentine, canvas, oils and paints. On every visit the walls quaked with Avant Gard ideas and Left Bank Exotica. It was a world apart from the science labs where Saskia spent her working days.

If only Alfie Collings hadn't been painting next to the massive Gothic window, life could have been so different. Tom told me with unusually emotive language how the summer sun dappled Alfie Collin's face and rinsed an exotic shine through his raven curls. 'Cherubic,' he described him. He also noticed deeply riveted lines across his forehead which he thought were rather too many for one so young although they highlighted his concentration. I could only imagine the things he didn't describe such as a peep of pink tongue accentuating absorption in his work, broad shoulders and long, artist's fingers which were destined to touch my daughter.

Apparently, it was some time before Alfie acknowledged their presence. Only when he changed the colour on his brush did he raise chocolate eyes in their direction. Did just a beat of interest register? Collar length hair definitely set him apart from college pupils, as did the tattoo of a serpent winding around his muscular left arm. He could never be mistaken for a member of the establishment.

Tom introduced himself and Saskia as they admired Alfie's massive canvas. Tom told me that, looking back, it was clear the crimson and black acrylic paint was of less interest to Saskia than the testosterone-fuelled young man. Isn't hindsight a wonderful thing?

'You're... um... our special prodigy,' started Tom, at a loss to name the boy. Tom was hopeless with names.

'Alfie', he enlightened him without eye contact.

'Ah yes, of course. Alfie. I'm Mr. Hanson and this is my daughter Saskia'.

'Dad has a terrible memory for names,' Saskia laughingly assured him. Clearly her father had embarrassed her.

'I hear you're making quite a name for yourself around here,' Tom offered. Apparently, Alfie didn't grace him with a reply. But he must have noticed Saskia. How could he not? She was so fresh in a light, flowery dress which slipped over her curves like silk under her denim jacket. Her copper hair probably caught the same shaft of sunlight that lit Alfie's masterpiece, competing for attention and winning hands down. He couldn't fail to catch her fragrance which would have overshadowed the smell of oils, clay and adolescent boy. But it was all water under a bloody crumbling bridge. How could we have been so stupid?

A few days after the devastating news of the pregnancy, I realised I had to re-engage in a difficult conversation with Tom, no matter how painful. I had to say that one little word. The same word we hadn't said often enough to Saskia. *'No. This baby will not be murdered in order to meet the exacting standards of Churchill's College.'* Hmm... no wonder I had a problem finding the right moment, but I had to muster courage.

The issue never deserted my brain, day or night. I knew I could deal with the scandal around college, although Tom probably wouldn't find it so easy. I had no idea, as he never talked about it. If someone in the establishment had challenged me about our daughter's behaviour, I'd have said 'fuck it' and been happy to move on. We always had options, even if the mother-in-law from hell was one of them. However, the one thing I was certain about was my already-violated daughter would not be scraped clean of a living, breathing baby. Not while I had breath in my own body. I thought maybe Mum and Dad would welcome her for the duration of her pregnancy but that felt like a retrograde step. It was half a century since pregnant girls were hidden in the countryside. I could see no easy solution, particularly as we were making decisions for a sixteen-year-old girl in a coma who had no idea she was pregnant.

The chemistry between Saskia and Alfie must have been rampant. I wasn't too old to remember first love and all its ramifications, the raging hormones and sleepless nights. Teddy Arnold was the dude of the whole year, but he never looked my way once. If he had, would I have offered up my virginity? Hmm...

I went over and over that chance meeting between Saskia and Alfie Collings and sometimes thought maybe I had spotted a flicker of something different in her eyes when they came home that day. But my imagination ran riot. Neither Tom nor I knew that she slipped back to the art room and presumably, that was the start of their relationship.

It couldn't have been more than a week after that chance meeting that she persuaded Tom to buy a piece of Alfie's work. 'Five hundred pounds is a snip', she told us. 'One should always buy art from up-and-coming artists. And still we didn't twig what was going on. Was life too busy for us to notice or did we have a rose-tinted view of our daughter? Had we excluded the possibility that a boy like him could interest her? Whatever was going on in our heads I don't know, but we bought a piece of his art and hung it in Saskia's bedroom. It was our money for that picture that he later used to pay for his party. The irony didn't escape us.

Over the weeks of misery, I questioned the way Tom and I had brought up our daughter. I asked myself the awkward questions, the ones no parent ever wants to hear the answer to. Did we ever say 'no' to Saskia about anything? Was she so spoiled that she didn't know the meaning of the word? I remember thinking at the time that the livid colours of Alfie's canvas clashed horribly with Saskia's girly bedroom, but she didn't agree. Of course she didn't. Tom waffled-on that she was only stamping her personality on her room, when actually she was probably already screwing him. No wonder we were racked with guilt.

But that crucial conversation could be put off no longer. Tom spoke to Mark Erdington to say we needed more time before we met to make decisions, and the baby issue was eating holes in us. Whatever happened to 'talking things over' or 'knowing what the other was thinking? It had darted like quicksilver from our marriage.

I suppose it was a blessing the boys had gone home for Easter. At least we weren't busy with school matters. It was always bitter-sweet when the holidays began but that term it couldn't come too soon. Tom still had plenty to occupy him, but it was easier to attract his attention during holiday time.

I booked a table in a restaurant renowned for passable food and asked for the 'snug table' which had a degree of privacy. It was the time and place to tell Tom how I felt about Saskia's baby. Even saying those words made my stomach churn but hopefully, being in a public place would keep things calm.

'We don't usually book here Snooks. Fancy a change, did you?'

'Well, I thought lunch out might be nice. It feels as if we're exhaling now that term has ended. You look tired, but I shouldn't even mention it I suppose; I looked in the mirror this morning and I know what a sight I look, too.'

'You look lovely as always, Snooks. Let's order, shall we?'

I decided to wait until the main course was served before I broached the subject. I reckoned a good mouthful of food would be sufficient to staunch any outpouring of anger, on either part. Even though I wasn't hungry, I ordered a steak which would concentrate my mind on chewing. Tom's filet of John Dory looked delicious but required considerably less attention than the content of my plate.

'It's time to let Mark Erdington know about the abortion Snooks. The sooner the better don't you think?'

'No!' It had gone from my mouth like a rifle shot and it was too late to redact it. 'What I mean is... we haven't made a decision yet and anyway...I don't think she should have a termination.' I spat the right words but didn't look at Tom's face.

There was silence. I'd become accustomed to dealing with silence in my counselling sessions; this was the kind that occurred when a curved ball was thrown to put one off -balance. But Saskia's baby was so much more than a curved ball.

'How can you even consider keeping this child?'

You'd have thought I'd suggested adopting a herd of delinquents.

'It's out of the question Lottie. You must know that.'

Tom was holding his knife and fork mid-air which was very frowned upon at Churchill's. I was determined to stand my ground.

'But I have a view too and I can't see this small life murdered because it's an inconvenience. Saskia was an inconvenience once. Have you thought of that?' I knew it was a low blow, but it was about to get dirtier.

'This isn't an 'inconvenience' Lottie. *This* is about to ruin our daughter's life. We have to act in her best interests.'

'And you know what that is, do you?'

'Of course I do. I'm her father.'

'And as her mother, I'm saying we have to consider waiting until she wakes, and then she can decide for herself. I'm not sure she'd want to scrape this baby into oblivion. Not sure at all.'

'Of course she would. She's not stupid Lottie. She'd see the folly of it. What about her medical career?'

'She was born an unwanted child who was given the chance to live. Don't you think that will influence her decision?'

Tom pushed his John Dory to one side. 'Hell's teeth Lottie! Listen to yourself. You're suggesting our daughter, who's made this one mistake, must carry the consequences for the rest of her life? This child won't ever go away if we allow her to have it. She'll be an unmarried mother with all the ramifications that entails. I have no idea where your head is these days.'

Ouch. Well, I thought, let's try this for size? I opened my mouth, and words tumbled like a waterfall. 'Let Saskia have the baby, and we can care for it while she goes to med school. Does that sound so bad?'

'God Lottie! Is that what this is all about? Our inability to have a child is impacting on our daughter. How can that be right?'

My steak went the same way as his John Dory. So much for calm. I sensed that if I wasn't careful, this would become a full-on slanging match and Tom wasn't into such behaviour, especially in public. He summoned the waitress and asked for the bill. No pudding then.

Uncharacteristically he didn't hold the door for me as we left which indicated the height of his anger. I was more than capable of dealing with a door and I stomped behind him to the car. As usual, I was thinking about Saskia. How the knife in her abdomen didn't harm the foetus I had no idea, but it was probably a sign that the baby was a fighter. It was a shrimp of matter with a fighting spirit, and I was damned if I'd let it down. We travelled home in silence.

Tom scraped a chair from under the kitchen table and told me to sit on it. I did my Steptford wife impression and stared out of the window where I noticed the wind had got the lilies. I should have tied them back. I noticed one in the corner by the fountain was the same pink as Saskia's favourite dress, but not as beautiful.

'Lottie, this nonsense has to stop.'

I was surprised he didn't bang his fist on the table. As I looked at Tom I wondered what the hell had happened to us. What had gone wrong with our marriage? Bloody Alfie Collings, that was what.

There was a flush on Tom's face and his eyes were fiery. I knew he meant business, but so did I.

'What appears to be nonsense to you could be of monumental importance to Saskia. Have you thought of that? Can you live with being called a murderer when she wakes up and finds out what you've done?'

'There's no way she'll want to be saddled with a child. You know that.'

'Actually, I don't.' I was icy cold and focused. It was as if everything that was important in my life depended on the next few minutes. 'I can't know what she wants any more than you can; this is life-changing stuff Tom, and I vote she's given the chance to make the choice. She may wake up next week to find we've had her womb scraped because it didn't suit us to nurture her baby.'

'And she may not.'

Below the belt, That was one nil to my husband. I struggled because nothing I said was sinking into his academic brain. I tried again. 'OK. Let's look at the worst scenario. Say she never wakes up.' An unattractive sniff escaped but hey, who cared? 'Let's say they want to switch off her life support machine. Well, they won't do that if she's carrying a baby will they. It could buy her some time.'

'What part of *ethical* does that argument fall into?'

'What part of family loyalty, loving and caring does your view fall into?'

'Lottie this has gone far enough.'

'No. Actually it hasn't. Think about this. If she never comes out of her coma, if we never have our daughter back, at least we will have her child. Her life won't have been in vain. Can you live with your decision if the worst happens?'

Tom left me seething to boiling point at the kitchen table. I heard his car engine and wondered where the hell he was going. He shouldn't have been driving in a temper, but I couldn't stop him. Actually, I wanted him as far away from me as possible.

I decided to go and see Saskia. I needed to tell her what was happening in case she could hear me. I imagined a squeeze from her hand. 'Squeeze once for yes,' I'd tell her. 'And twice for no, darling.' Hmm... like that was going to happen. I made a cup of tea to calm me down before I drove to the hospital. All the mugs were in the dishwasher, so I emptied it while the kettle boiled. The phone rang but I ignored it.

Parking at the hospital was the usual nightmare. I wasn't sure if I had enough small change so I asked a kindly gent if he could change a five-pound note. He was happy to oblige. It still meant putting a pound too much in the machine and of course, it never gave any bloody change. It must have owed us fifty pounds at least.

I took a couple of deep breaths after parking and made my way to Saskia's ward. Sister was on duty, and she smiled, 'Both of you today. Lucky Saskia.'

I gave her what I hoped was a smile, but it could have been more a grimace as I realised where Tom had disappeared to in his fury. I should have guessed. Oh well, I knew he wouldn't shout at me in front of Saskia, so I left the tin helmet at the door.

'Hi.' I spoke to Tom but my eyes were on our daughter.

'Hi Snooks. Come and sit down.' There was tenderness in his voice.

I walked to the other side of Saskia and held her hand and kissed her cheek. What I'd have given to see her green eyes sparkle with life. 'I need to change her underwear. Could you give us a minute?' I still hadn't looked at Tom. I dared not weaken.

'Of course. I'll get a cup of tea, shall I?'

'Not for me. I've just had one.' I pulled the curtains around her bed and busied myself. I noticed her hair needed brushing and I cleaned her mouth. When I'd finished I sprayed her with perfume and wondered if that was what bloody Alfie Collings found so irresistible. As Tom returned I swished the curtains against the wall and honoured my husband with a bleak smile.

'I've told her,' I lied. 'And she wants to keep it.' I engrossed myself in the poster that told me how to wash my hands. I knew I was playing dirty but there appeared to be no other way.

'I've just had a word with Sister.' Tom looked weary. Weary from the school term and no doubt weary of a wife causing problems. 'I mentioned we can't agree on the way forward and she suggests we involve Social Services. She said Saskia could be made a ward of court in the worst-case scenario. Can you bloody believe that?'

I couldn't but I grasped the news to my advantage. 'I think that might be a good idea.'

'Why would we want them involved for God's sake?'

I smiled despite my misery. Just the thought of Social Services calling at Churchill's College amused me. It had undoubtedly never been known and was beyond poor Tom's understanding. 'I've been doing some research,' I threw into the arena. 'We have to consider the rights of the unborn child. Did you know?'

'You're making this up Snooks. A bit low, don't you think?'

'How could you think I'd do that? The case is called the Frazer/Gillick competency. It's documented. Saskia's not the first underage girl in a coma to be pregnant.' My voice was rising until I remembered where we were. I whispered, 'it's true, I can give you the details if you want to read it for yourself.'

There was silence but I dealt with it. Great expense had been ploughed into my ability to deal with silence.

'No one else will make the bloody decision. That I can assure you.' Tom sounded as if he was addressing a class of boys.

'No one else as in *you*? Am I even on your radar?'

'No one else as in *us* Snooks. You know what I meant.'

And of course I did. But I'd learned years ago that when you can't compete on even terms with an academic, then you use instinct and emotion to find your way through the mire. I kissed my daughter and went home.

I had to play a dirty game to stop the massacre of a tiny life; I knew Tom would play the long game to get his way and it terrified me that I'd be unable to stop him. Of course, I recognised my personal experience of longing for a child was informing my stance. No surprises there. But I knew it was more than that. With therapy came awareness and I'd suddenly recognised that during our marriage I'd capitulated over every major family decision. And I knew that my acquiescence had sometimes been detrimental to happiness. I'd lost the feisty personality I brought to our relationship, something I'd put down to growing up and becoming a more responsible adult. Didn't everyone change after a few years of marriage? Had we become what Mum would call a 'marriage melded into comfortable togetherness?' Hmm... now that I was reflecting rather more than I used to, I was beginning to see a bullish side to my husband which wasn't attractive. Maybe the question I needed to ask myself was why had it taken such a monumental drama before I recognised it?

My life held more questions than answers and maybe I was picking at Tom because he was nearest to my anger. I needed to grasp reality before something else precious to me was damaged. But I was determined to hold firm on Saskia's baby. If she woke up and didn't want to keep the baby, then she would have options; if we washed it down the plughole while she slept, she'd have no options at all. Of course, I hadn't yet asked myself if I could love Alfie Collins baby. That was one step too far at that moment. And if the baby was born before Saskia woke, would I be ready for that?

I rang Social Services and then I lied to Tom. I told him they contacted us and wanted to discuss the baby. But when the woman from Social Services came to the house, I made sure it was only me who kept the appointment. Talking Tom out of being there was not hard. Social Services were anathema to him, not dissimilar to baby-snatchers or paedophiles. I still didn't believe he was acting in Saskia's best interests, and I was convinced his first loyalty was to Churchill's reputation.

I wanted to hate Miss Social Services, otherwise known as Maddie Frost, but it wasn't easy. She arrived with a smile and a briefcase and was young, pretty and polite. The most important thing was, after only five minutes in her company, I was convinced she had Saskia's interest at heart.

'It's not unusual for parents to disagree when a young girl gets pregnant. Often, they want different things but, of course, we have to make an informed decision about what your daughter would choose, if she was able. This case is an unusual one as Saskia can't convey her own view. It's so sad Lottie. I'll do everything I can to help.'

I believed she would.

*** 

### Tracey

Old Dickie rang the governor and said he needed to see Alfie 'cos *'his mother was worried about him.'* He was such a conniving bastard and convincing liar that they bought his story and gave him a visiting pass.

Dickie was sitting at a table in the Visiting Hall ogling McCarthy's missus when Alfie was let in.

'How's it hanging Old Man? Tired of shagging me mother yet?'

'Pity your mother didn't teach you some manners.'

'She did, but I save 'em for people that matter. Got any fags?'

Dickie ignored him.

'That girl's not good. Still in a coma, I heard.'

'Saskia. Her name's Saskia.' He glowered at Dickie like all his troubles were Dickie's fault. 'Shit. I need to get out of here. I need to see her.'

'Like the toffs will let you anywhere near her. Even if you could. You need yer head read if you think you can waltz in and see her.'

'What if she dies? What'll happen if she dies?

'You don't even want to go there. They'll have you fer murder.

Alfie ignored him. 'So, what's so important that you've come to see me? Come to gloat, have you?

'If you watch yer lip, I might be able to do you a favour. I just need a bit of information first. And don't tell me any bleeding lies, neither.'

'As if. So, what's on yer mind?'

'First of all, did you knife that posh kid?'

'Saskia. Her name's Saskia and no I didn't. I didn't push no E's on her either. Just vodka. And hell, did she like her first taste of vodka! I had to take the bottle off her. She was well gone.'

'So where was you when the knife thing started?'

'Drinkin' with mates. I didn't see it, but that bastard pushed her into the back room. Where they keep coats and stuff. First, I knew about it was when I heard her screaming. Bastard was trying to fuck her. Had her dress up and everything. And had a knife at her throat. Good nine inches it was.'

'I can't see much pleasure in 'forcing' a woman. Never did force a woman.'

'No, Old Man. You paid for it though, didn't you?'

'Nothing wrong with a little... arrangement. You'll see when you get a bit older.'

'Yeh, Right.'

'I heard your dabs was on the knife.'

'Yeh, but only 'cos I tried to stop the bastard from killing her. 'Corse it had me prints on it.'

Old Dickie made a play at digesting the facts. Thought he was a bleeding Judge. He still couldn't take his eyes off MacCarthy's missus. He was likely to get a doing over if McCarthy clocked it.

'Got a bloke what owes me a favour. He'll say he saw Ronnie Atkins attack the girl at your birthday bash. For the right sort of deal. Atkins is known fer drugs so the fuzz will put two and two together and make six. The best bit is he left the country yesterday for a few months in Morocco.'

'Right. Except it wasn't Atkins was it? It was Zillon Osborne. Big bloke...always hanging with that runt from Reading. The one that did time last year.'

Dickie seemed to be chewing on what Alfie told him.

'Spose we could finger him then. Leave it with me. I'll get a deal set up. We'll soon have you out of 'ere. Bye the way, got any problem with pervs? Any shower shenanigans?'

'Nothing I can't handle. Why?'

'It's just that I promised yer mother somebody on the wing would keep an eye on you. Like a son to me you are.'

'As if Old Man. As if.'

Dickie dug around in his pocket and passed a packet of twenty fags across the table. In a flash an officer was on Alfie with handcuffs at the ready.

'Get off me.' Alfie tried to flick him away. 'I haven't done nothing.'

'Don't touch a screw,' Dickie warned. 'He'll have yer.'

'Stand up Collins. Now.' A second officer appeared from nowhere. Then another. Some bastard must've called in the troops. Everybody was gawping.

'Hands behind your back.' Alfie obliged, more from panic than choice.

Dickie was ushered out and apparently you could hear him squealing as they took Alfie down to the Segregation Unit.

'Not exactly the shortest visit on record Collins, but close.' The Seg officer smiled like it was a big joke.

They put my Alfie in a cell block on the outskirts of the prison. Somewhere near the wire. He was still handcuffed. Bastards! There was no need for that. He didn't do nothing.

'First little visit to our hotel is it Collins? You'll find it very basic I'm afraid, but we do feed you.'

'Nobody told me I couldn't take smokes off an old man.'

'Well, you know now.'

And that was it. He was banged up in the Block and had to wait for a Governor to hand out his punishment. They only let you out of your cell for one hour a day in Segregation and then it's into a concrete yard. They told him he could be staying for a week or more. It was bollocks.

Alfie chucked his supper in the sink. Said it wasn't fit for a dog. Next day he could hear the officer outside jingling the keys before he was unlocked and then an officer told him the Governor wanted to see him. He got marched down the corridor and shoved in an office. Told to stand next to a desk.

'Name and number.'

'Collins. SD10943 AN.' He'd learnt that quick.

The Governor was a she-cat. Quite curvy but eyes that cut through you. A nurse appeared and sat next to Alfie. An officer told him to sit.

'Are the IMB coming?' the Governor asked an officer.

'No one is expected Governor.'

'Is Mr Collins fit for this adjudication, Nurse?'

'Yes Governor. Fit and well.'

Alfie looked at her and wondered how she knew if he was fit or not. He'd never seen her before.

'Collins,' the she-cat said, checking Alfie's notes. 'What made you think a visitor could pass things across in the Visit's Hall? You know the rules. They're up on the walls for everybody to read'

'No Miss. I never knew. Why can't an old bloke give me some smokes?'

'I ask the questions Collins. Got it?'

'Yes Miss.'

'It says on your records you were given a copy of rules and regulations in Reception. When you came in. Is that right?'

'Could've been Miss. I haven't read nothing yet. Only been in a week Miss. Me paperwork's still in me locker.'

'Ignorance of the rules is no excuse.'

'No Miss.'

'Officer Etchins, could you read Mr Collin's Wing Report please?

'Yes Governor. *At fourteen fifty-five yesterday Mr Collins was seen receiving a package from a visitor in the Visits Hall. It was passed across the table to him and he proceeded to place the package in his pocket. He was arrested and brought to Segregation. The package in question was a pack of twenty Rothman cigarettes. The Visitor was strip-searched on his way out of the Visitor's Hall but found to be carrying no other illegal items. Collins has been compliant since arrival and there are no previous nickings.'*

'Do you understand the charge Mr.Collins?

'Yes Miss.'

'And how do you plead to the charge Mr.Collins?'

'Guilty I 'spose Miss but I never knew it was wrong.'

'Can you read Collins?'

'Yes Miss.'

'Have you been made aware that there are prisoners on the wing who can help you read information and write letters?'

'No Miss.'

'Think hard before you answer my next question Mr. Collins. I'll ask you again. Have you been made aware that there are prisoners on the wing who can help you read information and write letters?'

'No Miss.'

'Officer Hanks, could you find out who was on duty when Mr Collins arrived and let me know.'

'Yes Governor.'

'Mr Collins. Because you pleaded guilty and you are in prison for the first time, I am prepared to give you the benefit of the doubt. Just for the record, you never pass anything between you and your visitors. Got it?'

'Yes Miss.'

'However, you cannot go unpunished.' She stopped talking; it was like those games shows where they keep you waiting for the answers. She wrote something on a piece of paper.

'OK Mr Collins. This is what I'm going to do. You'll get three days loss of canteen and you can return to the wing. Think yourself lucky you're not on closed visits for the next few months. And don't take me for a soft touch 'cos if you're up again, you won't be so lucky. Got it?

'Yes Miss.'

'And you do know that this prison becomes a non-smoking establishment next Monday, don't you?'

'No Miss.'

'Well, you can take my word for it. Better get to see a doctor and get some nicotine patches.'

'Yes Miss.'

Canteen was the only good thing in there. You could buy extra food and soap and stuff from the canteen. It was like a shop. And his smokes were gone, too.

'Shall I take him back to the wing Governor? Have you done?'

'More than done, Officer. How many more this morning?'

'Six Governor.'

'Let's get on, then.'

Officer Hanks took my Alfie back to his cell.

'Hand over your smokes Collins.' The screw watched as he dug them out of his locker.

'All of 'em.'

'That's it, Sir. Have a look. See? The screw checked his cell and then walked out with his ciggies. He was laughing, the bastard.

A bit later Alfie's cell door opened again.

'Here's your paperwork Collins. Make sure you read it this time.'

'I want to make a complaint.'

'Yeah, yeah. Everybody wants to complain about this place. Shut yer rattle and learn to follow the rules. That's good advice mate. Get it in your thick skull and things will go better for you.'

Alfie didn't answer. He sat on his metal bed and stared at the bog and decided then and there he was definitely going to cut himself before the trial.

\*\*\*

*Mummy, there are some things you should know... Alfie and me... we've been... doing it, you know. Having sex. He was careful not to push me 'cos he knew I'd not done it before. But I was ready and... I liked it. He was so gentle and we're in love... If you*

*knew him Mummy, really took the time to know him...
I'm sure you'd like him.*

## Lottie

I took Maddie Frost to see Saskia to ensure she knew
who I was agonising over. I wanted her to see Saskia
as a living, breathing young woman rather than
someone whose interests could be disregarded.
Sister offered us a small office for our meeting, and I
led Maddie into the cramped, windowless room.

'Have the medical team given you any indication
when Saskia may wake up?'

'The most hope we have is there doesn't appear to
be any brain damage. And her abdominal wound is
healing well. She's scarred, but it's healed OK.'

'I know very little about comas but I guess they can
last a fair while.'

'Umm....she could stay asleep right up until the
baby is born. If that happens, natural childbirth
would    be    unusual,    although    it    has    been
documented. The more likely route would be a C
section about four weeks before her due date.'

'What does your heart tell you Lottie? Have you any
idea what Saskia would want?'

'I only know what she wouldn't want. She was
illegitimate and we adopted her when she was two. I
think she'd want to give this baby the same chance
she had. Not to be scraped away before it has the
chance to live.'

'And if you're wrong? If she wakes up when she's seven months and doesn't want it?

'Then we'll deal with it. Better that, than she wakes up to find we've flipped a little life into the ether, don't you think?'

'You sound passionate about this Lottie. Is there any underlying issue that makes you feel so strongly?'

'I think I'm being a decent human being, and I'll make no apologies for that.'

There was a knock on the door and a nurse asked if we'd like a cup of tea. What a lifesaver. I could feel a wobble coming on and it wouldn't have looked very grown up if I'd cried. We talked some more about the legality of the situation.

'We could have Saskia made a ward of court to protect her interests, if we think you and Tom can't do so. If you stay opposed to each other's stance.'

I absorbed that snippet of information. It felt like blackmail to make one of us capitulate, but it also swung things in my favour.

'I don't think it will come to that. We need to talk some more and see if we can find some common ground.' I imagined Tom's face when I told him the decision could be taken out of our hands if he insisted on an abortion. I felt I had already won.

The weeks slipped by and Saskia still held on to her baby. I don't remember Tom and I discussing it again. There was acquiescence on his part and quiet jubilation on mine. I knew he would never allow a court to decide our daughter's future and surely common sense told him he couldn't win.

The summer term came and went, and the day of the trial loomed. No one was ready for it. Tom and I had fallen into a rhythm of barely speaking and certainly any scant conversation we had never moved far from 'steak or fish'. Looking back, I don't believe we had the mental or emotional resources to deal with our marriage, but maybe we should have found some.

Tom decided to mow the lawns the day before the court case, and I should have joined him in the garden to keep my mind off things. He was good at diverting his thoughts into something more useful than speculation, while I stressed over a mug of mint tea and stared into space. Enid had gone home, and the boys were away which left the house with an unsettling calm. The silence propagated my fears.

I watched the man I probably still loved stride across the grass with intent; up then down he walked creating a monotonous rhythm. The smell of new-mown grass wafted through the window and the gentle hum of the mower should have soothed me, but it didn't. I couldn't imagine feeling soothed until Saskia woke up. I saw the stripes on the lawn multiply with Tom's mechanical effort and submerged a desire to count them.

I decided to make a cottage pie for supper. At least it got me off the kitchen stool and away from my cold cup of mint tea. I thought we would both appreciate comfort food on the eve of the trial. The onions made a satisfying sizzle and I watched the meat cook as it changed from red to brown in the frying pan. The pungent aroma reminded me of childhood days when I watched Mum get supper at the farm. We didn't get many chances to eat cottage pie at Churchill's because life led us down a more sophisticated culinary route, but it was one of Saskia's favourite meals. As I thought about her, I convinced myself it was only the onions making me cry. The gin bottle was on standby.

When I thought about the nitty gritty of the procedure ahead of us, I could hardly comprehend how I would listen to days and days of evidence. It would be a bloodbath on the senses, and I knew I wasn't ready to hear about the misdemeanors of my daughter. And it was all due for public consumption because that little shit wouldn't plead guilty.

I knew I had to tell both my parents about Saskia's involvement with drugs, but it had been easier to shelve the decision until 'later'. However, when it was agreed they would attend court, I knew they'd hear all the gory details from someone else's mouth. Tom said I should have told them weeks before and he'd even offered to do it for me, but it would have been cowardly to duck the responsibility. Consequently, I did it at the eleventh hour.

My parents idolised Saskia. From the day she arrived as a cheeky toddler they embraced her as family. They'd watched her grow with unbridled pride and during her schooling at Cheltenham a deeper relationship with her had blossomed. But I needn't have worried. Dad's response was as cool as you like. 'You hear it all the time with those agricultural students,' he said. 'Drugs are everywhere. aren't they?' It was a huge relief when they both took it so well but how on earth would they cope with all the other things they were going to be exposed to? I had no idea.

I'd never been in a courtroom before, but on television programmes I'd noticed everyone dressed smartly and in sober mode. It was easy for Tom as any one of his work suits would do. I decided on my grey linen slacks which I was delighted to find were baggy and required a belt, a white blouse and no jewelry. I added a navy blazer as an option if the weather turned cooler. Everything was a blur, and I had the attention span of a gnat.

We'd decided Tom would be the one to give evidence while I sat in court with Mum or Dad. Tom said he would visit Saskia while I was in court, and I would see her when court was over for the day. I pondered the possibility that she would wake on the very first day of the trial and tell the court all about bloody Alfie Collins. But I knew the chances of that happening were only slightly higher than nil.

 'Any chance of some lemonade Snooks? It's hot as hell out there.'

Tom appeared in the kitchen, and I hadn't even noticed the silence of the mower. 'Sure. Let me wash the onion off my hands and I'll join you.' We sat by the window, each waiting for the other to speak.

'The hollyhocks have done well this year. They need a bit of weeding but they're a good six feet.'

I should have responded with an offer to weed, but I didn't.

'The gold price has gone up two percent today. Did you see the article in The Times? Good investment so far.'

As if I'd read the bloody paper and did I care about the price of gold? Instead, I wanted to yell at him about everything that was wrong with my life, but I didn't.

'It's lovely outside, darling. Fancy a bit of weeding?' Tom asked.

'I'm making cottage pie. Bit busy.'

'Thought I could smell something nice. Well, I'd better get on. Thanks for the drink.'

I watched him stride back to his lawnmower and I tried to recall those happy student days when he made my pulse race. But I couldn't. I tried to think of all the things we hadn't said to each other since Saskia slipped into a coma, but I couldn't manage that either.

The phone rang and it was Dad telling me he'd be with us by eight o'clock the next morning. I told him I'd have something nice for him to eat.

'Not a bad idea. Get something in the belly. An army marches on its belly,' he chuckled.

I smiled and realised I couldn't wait to see him. I needed his reassurance; I needed a hug and more than anything, I needed his support to see me through this ordeal. I intended to keep the news of the baby to myself for a while. There would be plenty of time for that conversation when Collins was sent to prison.

Dad had always been a stalwart with his down-to-earth logic, and it was good to know he'd be there. I wanted to smell that earthy scent of tweed jacket and see him remove his cap to expose a bald pate which was the only hairstyle I could remember. I wanted to be his little girl again.

The next day we woke up to wall-to-wall sunshine and no blazer was required. I'd promised Dad there would be food when he arrived around eight, and a full English breakfast fitted the bill. Enid had made sure everything was in the fridge to meet the demands of the largest appetite. I'd part-cooked the sausages while the bacon lay in limp, pink strips in readiness for the grill. I was expecting Tom to join Dad for breakfast although I didn't ask him if he was hungry. I would probably only manage to toy with a piece of toast.

I saw Dad's Land Rover come through our gates and a flutter of excitement made my heart race. I rushed to meet him while Tom took a more leisurely approach as he crossed the hall to open the door. I shot through the doorway to reach my Dad and shrieked with delight.

'Lottie, Lottie drives me potty.' He called as he locked his car and opened his arms as wide as a field gate. 'How's my lovely girl?' he asked as he swept me off my feet. You're a bit on the light side love. You need a bit of meat on those bones.'

I buried my face in the scent of him, just as I'd done as a child and wondered if I was using regression to cope with the stress. If that was the case, Nancy would be impressed by my self-awareness. I caught a shadow of disapproval from Tom which disappeared as quickly as it appeared. He was probably pleased no boys were around to witness my overt display of emotion. But I didn't care. I let the flow of love wash over me and wallowed in the arms of my dad.

Tom waited until Dad released me and then shook him by the hand. 'Welcome Eric. It seems too long since you were here. How's Stella?'

'Oh, you know. Well as can be expected, apart from the odd aches and pains. And... this of course. This coma thing has taken the stuffing out of us both.'

'Let's go inside. Lottie has a breakfast banquet prepared.'

I selfishly wanted a few minutes of Dad all to myself but that didn't happen. So, I busied myself in the kitchen while Tom and Dad talked about dairy herds and gardens.

'I hope you're joining us my girl, I see there's only two places laid for this feast.'

I glanced at the kitchen table and felt a flush of guilt that I wasn't even having a bacon sandwich. I knew an effort on my part would please both men in my life. 'I'll eat tonight. And I'll have some toast now.'

'No wonder you're like a rasher of wind. If you stand sideways, I can't see you.'

Dad smiled but his smile didn't quite reach his eyes. I knew he was worried about me, but I couldn't take on any more responsibility.

Tom made the coffee, and I buttered fresh bread for Dad to dip in his egg.

'One egg or two, boys?'

A chorus of 'two' sailed back and I wondered why men could fill their bellies in the face of conflict when women took a more apprehensive approach. I sat and kept the conversation flowing, hoping they would forget to watch how little I ate. A greedy Labrador at my feet would have been useful.

As Tom was to be a witness for the prosecution he was barred from the proceedings until after he'd given evidence. He looked like a lost little boy when Dad and I departed for court.

'Good luck, Snooks. I'll be with you every step of the way. Remember that.'

'Give Saskia a big hug and tell her I'll be in later.' I kissed him. I was sad Dad had to go straight home after the hearing as I knew he wanted to see Saskia, too. Tom promised to pick me up from the court when the day was done.

'And remember he's not worthy of your anger. He's nothing but a worm under your shoe, so how can he upset you?'

I wasn't sure I could follow that logic where Alfie Collins was concerned. The father of my grandchild sprang into my head, but I put on a brave face.

As Dad and I swept out of the driveway that morning I caught a smile from Tom which was intended to give me confidence to face the day. And maybe I saw regret that we'd rowed so badly in recent days. He'd told me the nightmare would soon be over, and I prayed he was right.

Churchill's College was so high profile that we were met on the court steps by a barrage of reporters and cameras. Also waiting for us was a police family liaison officer called Karen who had called on us a couple of times. Dad was almost frozen with fear by the scrum, and I heard myself encouraging him to get inside.

'It's ghastly isn't it? Karen looked calm and had probably seen it all before. 'Try to think of the benefits they offer when they get the story right.'

I'd made a point of not reading the papers for weeks and I couldn't imagine I would read the court reports either. I introduced Dad to Karen, and we were ushered into the court room where seats were found for us.

'I'm not staying for the hearing, but I'll come back at lunchtime to make sure you're OK.' Karen was carrying a bulging briefcase and had the look of a busy woman. I thanked her and absorbed the alien world we'd landed in.

I noticed the long, polished benches which I guessed were for the jury and I stared at the dock. I knew from the moment Alfie Collins entered the courtroom he would become real; he'd be etched on my mind for the rest of my life. No longer a faceless hooligan, he'd be a criminal, a man who nearly killed our daughter. I'd endured months of Alfie Collins festering in my brain, and I was a shadow of the woman I wanted to be. Instead, I was the woman who took comfort from stabbing a voodoo doll with Saskia's school compass to vent my anger on a ruffian from a sink-estate family. But I knew it was too easy to hide behind a safety blanket of ignorance, to fall into denial about Saskia's culpability. She must, undoubtedly, take a portion of blame.

I looked around as the court filled up and wondered about the jury; they'd be ordinary people I could have seen in Waitrose. Dad took my hand which made me want to cry. How ridiculous was that? I knew the blanket of anonymity was about to be whipped away like a layer of skin, but I didn't feel ready. Collins would be there in the flesh in a couple of minutes; his eyes, his hair and his skin would be forever tattooed on my brain. We'd breathe the same air. I'd shroud him in my cloud of anger and when I looked him in the eye, he'd know I hated him. But that wouldn't hurt him would it? I knew hate had no healing qualities.

And it wasn't only me who was racked with fear. That morning Tom had paced while drinking his morning coffee and was short with me over bathroom preferences. But he, of course, was true to his tradition and mustered a strategy to deal with the day. Coping was probably written into his DNA. He lived on a cerebral plane which, at that moment, appeared so much more attractive than my lot in life, particularly while I was perched with my Dad on this emotional slag-heap. I made a note to try harder.

In my mind it was a no-brainer that Collins would be found guilty, and it was the only verdict I'd considered. I longed for Saskia to wake up because maybe, just maybe, that would soften my stance towards Alfie Collins. I didn't want to carry so much hate around. I was bowed with the burden. But still my daughter lay in silent repose, offering no more than the occasional flutter of her eyelids.

The one bright spot in my life was that I'd managed to keep Saskia's baby cradled in her womb. Through my cajoling and long silences, Tom hadn't found the courage to insist upon an abortion. And I'd been sneaky. I'd left nothing to chance. A few days before the court hearing I'd sourced a specialist charity who gave me impartial advice about our situation. I was able to raise all my issues such as conception from rape and what Saskia's wishes might be if she wasn't in a coma. But was it rape? I liked to imagine it was, but I couldn't erase the memory of how happy my daughter was during those weeks when she must have been meeting Collins. Facing unattractive truths was stressful and it was the imagined detail I teased from within the knot of turmoil that crippled me. I was grateful to the anonymous lady who listened to my grief. She'd gently steered the conversation to deal with what I knew, rather than those things I supposed to be true. And the rights of the unborn child gave me hope. I knew about the problems facing medical staff when two parents had polar opinions and from what I'd read, common sense usually prevailed. Alleluia.

***

## Tracey

I'd had to cancel work 'cos of going to court and had no idea what we'd live on. It could have gone on for a week or more and I had to be there for Alfie. I needed extra allowances to see me over the court case which meant queuing down the social and telling some stranger all our family business.

Mum said she'd have Lily while I was in court, which was a first.

'I'll give her a bit of dinner,' she said. You pick her up when yer ready love. We'll probably go to the park most days.'

It was just my luck the court case cropped up in school holidays, but I had no idea what had got into my mother with her offer to help.

'That lad of yours will probably get what's coming to him.' She pursed her lips like a pantomime dame. 'Can't see him getting away with it.'

She thought she was bloody mystic Meg, my mother. *'That lad of yours?'* Whatever happened to *'my grandson*?' She sounded like she'd already disowned Alfie. And as if I didn't know what was gonna happen to my boy. I didn't need reminding.

I'd told Lily about her brother. It wasn't easy, but I had to do it before some kid told her about all the shenanigans. Kids do a lot of earwigging into adult conversations so I had to tell her he might go to prison for a long time. She cried a bit and wanted to know what it would be like in there. And she said she wanted to visit him, but I wasn't sure about that. Prison wasn't any place for my Lily.

I heard a key in the door and my stomach flipped 'cos for one second, I thought it might be Alfie. Stupid. Quick enough I realised it was Dickie.

'All right are you, ducks?'

'What do you think?'

'Now, now. No good looking on the black side. He might get off.'

'Cows might bleeding fly.'

He settled himself on the sofa without asking. 'Need any help with Lily? Like me to come to court with you?'

I shook my head. 'I'm OK on my own.

'Sure you are, ducks. Never let anybody close, do you?'

'All them years on the game, I 'spect. Ring any bells?' I looked at him like thunder and wished he'd piss off out of our lives, but I knew he never would. They'd take him out of Skankland in a box.

'I've got to get down the social to see about some money to cover the court case. Could go on for days. Shan't be able to work.'

'Why ain't you giving evidence?'

'No need. That do-gooder from the youth club offered. Seems she thinks Alfie's a 'talented man'. Yeh right. Don't take talent to get put inside.'

'Must say I'm a bit surprised.'

'What? That I'm not giving evidence? She'll do a better job than me. I'd get all tongue-tied with nerves if they put me in the witness box.'

'Your trouble is you always look on the dark side of life, Trace.'

'P'raps that's cos it's the only side I know. Anyway, I gotta get on. See yerself out.'

As I walked to the bus stop, I wondered what my Alfie was thinking. How was he feeling? Hours and hours locked in a cell made time for a lot of thinking. He must have known he would probably go down although he could be pretty cocky when he wanted. I hoped he wouldn't be cocky in the witness box.

Trouble never seemed to leave my doorstep. I'd had a phone call from the screws a few days before to say they'd moved Alfie onto a different wing 'cos the silly bugger had cut his wrists. I nearly wet myself when they told me. I couldn't believe Alfie would be so stupid. He's not the type. Then the penny dropped, and I realised what his 'slicer' was for. I imagined all sorts of awful things and wondered if it was bad enough for me to lose my boy.

I went to see him in the hospital wing and the little bugger had a grin on his face from ear to ear. And there was me thinking he was at death's door. I couldn't have a go at him with all the screws about, but I wanted to clip his ear. Apparently, he never meant to kill himself, it was all a bit of shenanigans. He'd been told they'd move him to the vulnerable prisoner's wing if he tried to cut himself. They said life was less violent in there.

I was mighty relieved when I found out the truth of the matter, but I'd still have had a go at him for being so stupid. What if it had gone wrong? Trouble was, he had such a way with him it was hard to be angry for long.

Sometimes, I thought Alfie could have made it in the movies with a bit of a break. Face of an angel, Annie Etheridge always said. Girls couldn't resist him, even that posh girl who was no better than the slappers round our way, went with him.

There was a queue at the social and I stood next to a woman who smelled like a polecat. I can't stand dirty people and I let the bloke behind me go in front.

'Thanks love.' When I looked at him, he winked, and I knew I'd seen him before. I was trying to work out where I knew him from when he touched my arm.

'Did you ever go back and get your GCSE's Trace?'

It was the voice, I think, that gave him away. 'Alan Curtis? Bloody hell. Thought you went in the army.'

'I did, but I'm out now. Did fifteen years. That was enough. What you been up to? How's your Alfie?'

Where to start? I couldn't think of anything to say and the next thing I knew I was crying. Not a little sniff, but a flood of snot and tears that seemed to come from nowhere.

'Hey Trace. No need for that, is there?'

He put an arm round my shoulder which made matters worse.

'Move up love. Yer holding up the queue.' A miserable old git three behind me started fussing.

'Do you mind? Can't you see the lady's upset?'

'Tears won't pay my phone bill nor buy me ciggies.'

'She don't look like a lady from where I'm standing.'

Alan looked like he might clobber a bloke with two nose-rings who was mouthing off, but the next thing I knew we were out the door.

'I gotta get some money... I need....'

'You don't need nothing if you're a friend of Alan Curtis, Trace. Come on.'

I sat in his car and kept crying. It felt like I'd never stop. 'I'm not a baby, honest.'

'Gutsy more like. You were always gutsy. Keeping your Alfie was gutsy.'

I kept hearing the word gutsy in me head. Gutsy... gutsy... it was going round and round like a tumble dryer.

'Look after his mum does young Alfie? What's he now – seventeen, eighteen?'

I cried a bit more, but I didn't tell him about my Alfie. And I didn't tell him about Lily either. Even when he dropped me home.

I'd just finished ironing Lily's clothes that same evening when there was a knock at the door. I hoped it wasn't Dickie who'd forgotten his key and had come to have another go at me. I needed time to think about it all, to weigh up the pros and cons before getting knee-deep in drugs and something I had no control over. I'd done that too many times in my life. But Lily answered it before I had time to think and she came into the kitchen with a funny look on her face.

'Mum, it's a man.'

She scarpered past me to go back to her tele programme.

'Hiya Trace. Can I come in a minute?'

I was a bit taken aback to be honest. I stood aside and he came right into the sitting room.

'Hello. And who are you then?'

'I'm Lily. Do you like The Simpsons?'

'I do. I've come to have a chat with yer Mum.'

I nodded him into the kitchen. 'Tea?'

'Why not?'

I put the kettle on and tried to get a quick look at him as he sat down.

'How long you been here then?'

'Too bloody long. Where you living?'

'My Gramps left me a small house in Durnford Road when he died about five years ago. I've been letting it out until I finished. In the army. I'm with Mum for another couple of weeks, then I move in.'

'Blimey. You did alright.'

'I loved the old man, Trace. He always told me I'd get the house when he died. Not sure I thought much about it 'til he went. It's nothing posh, but I'm lucky. Lucky to have my own place.'

I swilled the tea bags round the mugs and slopped milk in. Alan got up and carried them to the table.

'What you doin' fer a job now you're out?'

'Had a bit of luck there, too.' He slurped his tea which must have been scolding hot. 'I start at Reynolds Transport on the industrial estate in three weeks' time. I learned a trade in the army and I'm lucky... picking up a job quick. Got a foreman's job.'

'Good for you.' I wondered why he'd come, but it seemed a bit rude to ask.

'Had to sign on for six weeks when I came out. Lucky, as I wouldn't have bumped into you.'

'Oh. Yes. Lucky.'

'What you up to then Trace? I heard about your Alfie from Mum. Is that what all the tears were about earlier? Why didn't you tell me?'

I didn't know what to say. 'Might have been. Not sure I know, really.'

I remembered Alan used to have a stutter and everyone used to tease him. I wanted to ask about his stutter but that seemed rude, too. After we'd drunk the tea and caught up a bit, he dug around in his pocket like he'd lost his hankie.

'Here. This'll tide you over.'

It was an open envelope, and it was stuffed with notes.

'It's five hundred quid Trace and I don't want it back.'

I pushed the envelope across the table. 'I ain't a charity case.'

'Never said you were, but everybody needs a leg up at one time or another. Are you telling me you can manage? Course you can't.'

No, I bloody well couldn't but I knew what would come next. As Mum always said, '*there's no such thing as a free dinner.*'

Alan got up and put the kettle on again. 'I'll take you for a pint tonight, if you fancy it.'

He made another brew, moving round my kitchen like he'd been there before.

'Can't. I've got Lily.'

'How about we go to the Plough on Sunday then? All of us. Have a bit of dinner? The play area's good there for little kids.'

What was it with him? He never took any notice of me when we were at school, and I hadn't improved with keeping. I knew the Plough was posh. I pretended to think about it but really, I was wondering if I had something to wear. 'Alright then. I can't pay and you ain't getting nothing else. No funny business. Understood?'

He actually laughed at me like I was funny. 'Still feisty then Trace? I'll be paying and you and Lily will be eating. And no funny business, as you put it. I'll pick you up at twelve.'

He got up and he was still chuckling. I watched to see if he picked up the envelope with the money in it.

'Tell you what Trace, you use this as a leg up and pay me back if you can. OK?'

I nodded. I stood at the kitchen window and watched his car disappear. I couldn't help a little smile. 'Lily, we're going out proper posh on Sunday.'

***

*Mummy. Help me get back to you and Daddy...Please.*

## Lottie

We waited for something to happen while Dad looked around the court room as if he'd been dropped on Mars.

'Did Mum get her dentures sorted? She was really stressed about them when I spoke to her.'

Dad chuckled. 'She did. What she was stressing about was going to WI without them. You know she cares what everybody thinks. Bugger if I'd care, but your Mum's different. You know that.'

Butterflies had infested my body. I allowed my eyes to focus on the empty jury seats and guessed the judge would appear from the central door on the paneled wall. The craftsmanship from years gone by engrossed me and I wondered how long it would be before it was ripped out in the name of progress.

Seats filled up around us and the buzz of conversation reminded me of waiting for a Christmas pantomime to begin. Mum took me to Cheltenham to see the pantomimes when I was a child, and I loved the sequins and rude jokes. But I was always nervous while we waited for it to start because I thought we might have come on the wrong day or maybe it had been cancelled. Silly child. But one thing was certain about the court case, it wouldn't be cancelled and there'd be no jokes.

The reporters were chatting amongst themselves, and I wondered if the case would get as far as the Wilts and Glos weekly rag. I decided it was unlikely, unless any reporters twigged my hometown was Cirencester. Someone told me they liked to do that sort of thing; it earned Brownie points if they tipped off a colleague about a person's connection to another area. I hoped for Mum and Dad's sakes they wouldn't make the connection.

I tried to guess where the little shit's family were sitting and realised if they were behind me, then I had no chance to identify them. Either his mother or father must be black, but I could see only white people around.

Suddenly the court was told to rise, and I tried to still my heartbeat. My mouth was desiccated but my hands were slicked with sweat. How does that work? But before I found an answer to the workings of my body, there was a shuffling around me which suggested the event was about to unfold. The court staff bowed as the judge took her seat on a raised plinth while the jury filed into their seats in an orderly line. It was impossible to guess characters or dispositions from their appearance, but I prayed they would deliver the right verdict.

Then *he* arrived - my nemesis. A yob by the name of Alfie Collins rose from steps behind the dock and I was riveted by his appearance. He wore a smart grey suit with a blue polka-dot tie and his glossy hair was brushed to perfection. There was a male officer beside him, but Alfie wasn't handcuffed although he looked scared, which I found oddly comforting. His black hair sat on his collar and had a gentle curl any girl would be proud of; his skin was pale, milk chocolate. I noticed he was tall and broad-shouldered as he stood in the dock and... I grudgingly had to admit he was attractive. A small, mousy woman on the end of our row started to cry when he appeared but she didn't look old enough to be his mother.

The prosecution laid before us a scenario of which much was surmised. No one could know the full truth until my baby woke up. I heard sentences such as 'and was a young innocent girl from a good family entirely to blame for ending up at a drug-fueled party?'

*Of course not. That was my fault.*

'The prosecution witness will say she was coerced to attend a party by the man you see in the dock, ladies and gentlemen of the jury. This is the man who was heard to threaten her with a knife, before stabbing her.'

This was already too much to bear, and I had no idea how I'd cope with the coming days. I wished I'd brought a bottle of water. Dad squeezed my hand which nearly brought a cloudburst of tears and all I could think of was how scared Saskia must have been. The barrister's voice continued like a bee in a jam-jar.

'You will hear how this same man was seen leaving the scene wearing blood-stained clothing. You will hear how his fingerprints were found on the knife. And you will hear, also, how the young girl is still in a coma; her condition caused by the consumption of drugs and injuries the prosecution witness will say was inflicted by this man.'

I zoned out. It was an ability I'd learned years before, but it could catch me out when I missed chunks of conversation. Sometimes, it saved me from things I didn't want to hear.

They called the caretaker of the premises to give evidence, and he confirmed what I already knew. Alfie bloody Collins was to blame. He told the court that alcohol and drugs were forbidden on the premises, so why, I whispered to Dad, didn't he do his job and keep my Saskia safe? He said he saw blood on Saskia's clothing, and he saw the knife. I felt crumpled by the words floating around the court.

I noticed people pouring coffee from flasks as if they were there for the spectacle. It seemed that life continued all around us, for everyone else, but not for Dad and me. I felt stranded in a bubble while I waited for justice to be carried out.

The jury were attentive. I wondered what they did for a living and if any had a sixteen-year-old daughter who'd deceived them. Of course they hadn't.

Lunch was a sandwich more suited to feeding ducks. Dad and I hardly referred to the hearing while we munched, preferring to malign the meagre content of our sandwiches. Karen didn't show, but I didn't care. I watched all those people who didn't have a child lying in a coma and envied them their freedom from the misery that was ours. The coffee shop failed dismally to satisfy my need for a strong gin and tonic; instead, we made do with well-stewed tea which Dad loaded with sugar because Mum wasn't there to stop him.

Dad and I took our seats for the afternoon session and the proceedings dragged on with little else of note revealed. A member of the jury nodded off around three o'clock; he was probably a victim of the stifling heat. I watched the smart lady next to him poke him awake, which would have been amusing on any other occasion.

Eventually, I joined Tom who was waiting outside in the car, as arranged, and before I was ready to say goodbye to him, Dad kissed me and wished us luck. He confirmed Mum was on her way and needed to be met off the five o'clock train.

'How was it Snooks? You looked bushed.' Tom put his hand on my shoulder. I had no idea how I was, but I didn't want to fall into his arms. I wanted my dad. I must have offered some platitude to satisfy Tom.

'Saw a lot of people coming out. Was the court full?'

'It was. And so hot. I must remember to take water tomorrow.'

'Was Eric OK? Don't expect it was easy for him hear the evidence.'

'He was a stalwart. The only problem was his bladder. I'm wondering if he's got prostate problems. Bless him. It was almost funny to see him squeeze along the row so many times. And so full of apologies.'

'Do you think they'll nail him? Collins?'

'It's too early to say, but there's plenty of evidence against him.'

'What did you think of him?'

'I expected a tough looking yob and saw a prospective lawyer. He was so spruced up it was a shock.'

'Easy to put on a suit Darling, but it doesn't make him any less guilty, does it?'

'How was Saskia?'

'Peaceful. They'd bathed her and she looked beautiful. Shall we pick Mum and up then go straight to see her? We could eat out.'

'Good idea.' To be honest, I had no idea how food entered Tom's head, but I was happy to push a few bits around a plate and Mum might be hungry.

The train was fifteen minutes late and Mum was flustered because she'd caused us 'inconvenience'.

'It's not a problem, Mum. Honestly. How was the journey?' I gave her a hug, but it didn't ooze the essence of revival I'd squeezed from my dad.

Our daughter was in her pink tracksuit bottoms and a white tee-shirt announcing 'Live a Little' in gold letters. The irony was not lost on us. I had clean clothes for her, and I changed her socks for her favourite Micky Mouse pair. When I'd finished, Mum and I sat either side of her and Mum tentatively held her hand. I noticed the incongruity of her old lady's skin entwined with the perfect skin of my daughter.

I didn't tell Saskia I'd been to court and had my first siting of the monster who'd damaged her; I told her we were going to take our holiday in Cornwall when she woke. Hurry up, I urged her. I reminded her of the walk on Sennen beach and the pasties she loved.

I felt drained after my day in court, and we only stayed with our daughter for a short while. I kissed her and told her we'd be in again the next day.

'Shall we try Pizza Express, Snooks?'

I was shocked at Tom's suggestion; I was sure he'd never graced a Pizza Express in his life. 'Fine. Is it OK with you Mum? Pizza? It should be quick at this time, and no college boys around either.' I wasn't fussed what we ate, and Mum seemed happy to eat anything, too.

Over supper Mum announced that she intended to stay until the trial was over. Apparently, it was all arranged, and a neighbour was going to keep an eye on Dad. She'd made sure there was enough to eat in the freezer and had given Dad a lesson on how to use the microwave. It was going to be a mixed blessing for me as I had no spare emotional capacity to give her.

When we got home, Mum wanted to unpack her things and have an early night. I kissed her after making sure she had a glass of water to take her pills. 'Sleep well.'

'I always do love. Only the wicked can't sleep!'

When I went into the drawing room Tom had already poured gin and tonics. 'I had no idea she'd be staying so long.' I gulped at my gin. 'I'm not sure I can cope with Mum as well as everything else.

'She wants to look after you. We all do. Let us both spoil you for a change.'

Over our cocktails Tom told me he'd picked up bits of gossip from Enid who apparently lived close to Alfie Collin's grandmother. Enid told Tom there was no father on the scene and the mother was a child when she had him. So, it could have been her sitting at the end of the row. How grim.

***

## Tracey

'Can I wear my princess dress Mum?'

I had to think about it 'cos I had no idea what people wore out for Sunday dinner. I told her it would be fine. It was one less thing to worry about. I changed my own outfit about four times and still couldn't decide what to wear. It was warm so I didn't need a coat which was lucky 'cos I only had an old mac or my hoodie. I'd been to a charity shop and found a dress with a tie belt which I hoped would flatter my figure, without being showy

I noticed in the mirror that a few days of sun had brought out my freckles, but it couldn't be helped. I'd raided Mum's makeup when I fetched Lily on Friday, and used her concealer and pink lipstick. I'd got my own mascara and reckoned that was all I needed. Lily had given me some perfume for my birthday, so a squirt of that boosted my confidence a bit. It was a funny feeling, having a bloke take an interest in me when it wasn't for sex. I could get to like it.

Lily looked fantastic. She was as pretty as a picture, and she handed me her hairbrush with instruction that she wasn't having plaits, and she wasn't having a ponytail.

'Too much like school. Did you ever see a princess with plaits?'

'No. I don't believe I did.'

I brushed her soft blonde hair until it shone and persuaded her that princesses wore Alice bands.

She was really excited and kept getting in my way when I tried to use the mirror.

'Sit and watch tele so you don't get dirty.'

'TV is boring. Can I watch a DVD?'

Anything was OK as long as she gave me a bit of peace to get ready.

I'd been thinking about Alan Curtis off and on. I asked Mum what she knew about him, and she hadn't heard anything for years. She knew his Gramp died, but nothing else. Part of me didn't think I should go out with him while my Alfie was locked up. But it was a real treat for Lily, so I was swayed. I told her I wanted her on best behaviour, and she asked if Alan was my boyfriend. I told her I didn't want to hear such nonsense.

I watched Alan as he parked his car and decided he wasn't half bad. The day I'd sniveled all over him, I hadn't got a proper look, and I'd felt shy when he plonked himself in my kitchen so didn't dare do much looking then, either. But he was tall; he must have been six foot. And smart, too. He'd got nice jeans on and a black shirt. His hair was short, and you could guess he'd been in the army.

He knocked on the door.

'I'll go. I'll go.' Lily raced to open it and I heard him admire her princess dress. 'Father Christmas gave it to me, but I've never worn it outside. Only in the house.'

I smiled. She'd probably have told him her life history, if he asked.

'Hi Trace. You look nice.'

I was a bit lost for words. 'Er... thanks. You look nice too.' What a daft thing to say to a bloke.

'I've booked a table for one o'clock so there's time to sit outside with a drink first.'

'How do you book a table?' Lily was a nosey little madam. She always had to know everything.

'Well, when you take a princess and her Mum out, you need to be sure there'll be a special table for them. So, you ring up and organise it, then no one else can sit there.'

'Wow. Cool.'

We both laughed and it broke the ice.

'Come on then. Your car awaits. Princesses go first.'

I suddenly wondered why he wasn't married. I'd not thought about it before, but I decided he probably was. Wouldn't that be just my luck? He was a good talker. I didn't have to say much to start with. Between him and Lily, they talked for England.

We drove to the Plough which was about three miles away. I used to think I'd have liked to work there when I was at school, but I never did. But if I'd had to choose between working at the Plough and having my Alfie, I'd definitely have gone for Alfie.

The car park was nearly full, even though we were early. Lily was beside herself with excitement and kept trying to point out empty parking spaces.

'Leave it to Alan love. He'll find somewhere.'

As I let Lily out of the back seat I was suddenly nervous. My stomach churned but there was no time to think because Lily ran off shouting, 'over here. The door's over here.' I smiled at Alan who looked amused, and I wondered if he'd got any kids. He seemed to have a way with them.

Alan opened the door and let us in, and I told Lily to stay right next to me. Her eyes were all over the place and I wasn't much better. I was right, all those years ago – it was posh.

'Shall we have a drink in the garden?'

We opened the door into a huge leafy space and found a bench in the shade, which pleased me. The sun always made me red and blotchy. I sat down while Lily ran off to play with some children and Alan disappeared with our drinks order. I thought to myself that if I hadn't had Alfie so young, this could have been my life. I could have had a nice bloke, and enough money to eat at posh places. But I didn't have long to think about it 'cos Alan appeared with drinks and Lily came running back to claim hers.

'Look Mum. Can I go on the slide?

We watched as she tried out all the play stuff and I sipped a half of beer, smiling at her. It wasn't often we got to have fun together.

'I like this place. I've got a nipper of my own and she likes to come here. I only have her every other weekend though.'

So, he had been married. And had a kid. I was tongue-tied so I never asked any questions. When we'd finished our drinks, Alan said we should claim our table. I lured Lily inside with the promise of ice cream if she ate her dinner.

'The table is in the name of Curtis', he said, calm as you like.

A waitress led us to a table for four by the window.

'Someone will take your drinks order Sir.' She handed us all a menu. Even Lily got one.

'Can I have anything I want?'

I gave her one of my looks and she went quiet.

'Nice place,' I said. I wished I'd put on a bit more makeup.

'The important thing is the food's always good, Trace.

I'd read in one of those trashy magazines that the girls left lying around in the factory, if you're nervous on a date, always ask the bloke something about himself. So, I went for it. 'Why haven't I seen you about fer years?' I lowered my eyes to the menu while he answered.

'I've been back from time to time. We just haven't seen each other. I joined the REME at sixteen and I've served overseas quite a lot.'

'What's the REME?' Lily was all bright-eyed and I shot her a 'good behaviour' look.

'I used to mend lorries and tanks in the army. We kept the army going,' he said with a chuckle. Seen anything you like on the menu Lily?'

'I can read now, you know.'

'You look like a smart kid to me. Have you seen the children's menu on the back? Bet there's something you'd like on that.'

I was thinking he was too good to be true and waited for the bombshell. 'So, what did your missus think about you being away so much?' I thought that would sort it.

'Ah.' He smiled. 'Not a pretty story, that.'

I decided to have the roast dinner 'cos I could never afford to cook a roast at home.

'She buggered off after thirteen months.' Alan looked me straight in the eye. 'Said she felt like a war widow, and she divorced me in under two years. Not exactly the fastest divorce on record but getting that way.'

'Haven't you bothered since?' Hope there's not a girlfriend gunna pull my hair out.'

'Oh Trace. What sort of life have you been living?'

'You don't want to know,' I muttered and pretended to be choosing from the menu. The waiter brought a rum and coke for me and another beer for Alan. Lily looked as proud as punch with her orange juice and lemonade which had ice and a straw in it.

'Can I have another if I want?'

'Ssh. Watch yer manners.' I noticed Alan was still smiling.

The dinner was fantastic. I had roast beef, the same as Alan, and Lily ordered sausage and chips. She asked the waitress if they had tomato sauce and grinned when they put a bottle on the table and left it within her reach. 'I'll put the sauce on,' I told her. I was imagining it going everywhere.

So...he wasn't married, he liked kids, and he didn't seem to have heard any tittle tattle about me. So far so good, I thought. But I knew it would end in tears, cos that's how my life was. But I decided I might as well enjoy it while I could. And I was gonna have a pudding, too.

***

*Mummy... there's one thing I keep thinking about. I'm not really sure how to say it but... I wonder, if you and Daddy hadn't adopted me, would I have grown up in a family like Alfie's? Do you think, perhaps...? I belong with Alfie. Could he be the right sort of boy for me?*

**Lottie**

The trial was concluding, but we were still living with the nightmare of it. I was convinced Alfie Collins was going to prison and I couldn't wait for it to be over. After Tom had given evidence, we alternated the days in court. One spent time with our daughter and one stared at the monster who'd broken our lives.

I tried to keep busy and one morning I decided to catch up on some chores; the sort of things Enid never had time to do. I had my head in the airing cupboard sorting the abundance of linen when I heard the phone ring. I knew Enid was around, but she hadn't heard it and Mum was in court with Tom. I eventually caught the insistent ring.

'Lottie? Is that Lottie?'

My throat was dry, and I coughed before answering. 'It is. Hello.' I knew it was Mark Erdington. He had a distinctive voice and when you'd imagined that call for as long as we had, the shock was palpable. Is Saskia dead? Are they going to switch off her life support? My mind was already in overdrive, but I verbalised none of my jumbled thoughts, I just listened for the news that would surely impact on the rest of our lives.

'Hello Lottie. Mark here. I'd like you and Tom to come in. If you can come right away, so much the better, but I could see you this afternoon, too.'

I didn't make a sound. The hideousness of the situation rendered me devoid of speech.

'We believe Saskia is in the first stages of waking... Lottie are you still there? Her vital signs suggest a level of consciousness we've not seen, and she's opened her eyes a couple of times. Can you get here fairly soon?'

'Of course... of course. I'm sorry. I'm such a mess, and... I was expecting the worst.'

'Is Tom at home?'

'He's in court but I'll contact him, and we'll be straight there. Thanks. Thank you for calling. We'll see you soon.'

Enid appeared from somewhere and took the phone from my hand. 'Shall I try to contact Mr Hanson?'

'No, it's OK Enid. I'll contact the court and get a message to him.'

Tom insisted on driving while Mum and I made the journey to the hospital in silence. I did some deep breathing and convinced myself I would handle the next few hours with dignity, no matter what the outcome.

'It's funny,' Tom said as I stared at the road like a robot. 'You wait and wait, and then when it happens you feel like a fish out of water. Do you feel like that Snooks?'

I had no idea how I felt other than scared witless and pleased Tom was by my side. Mum, bless her, had nothing to say but was probably mirroring my feelings. I felt a ray of hope, although it wasn't very bright; hope hadn't shown its face in a while. Hope had been diminished by the enemy, better known as fear. But I was determined to stay strong and the time for tears was over. I prayed I could live up to my resolve and push aside all negative thoughts although it wasn't easy.

'It looks hopeful Snooks. But we mustn't get carried away. Small steps I think, that's what's needed. Who rang? His secretary'

'No, Mark rang. He wanted to give us the news himself. She still wasn't conscious when he rang but they obviously expect her to wake, from the way he was talking.'

After weeks of waiting for news, I was petrified. Words stumbled around my mouth, and I expected my legs to let me down. But it was time to buck up and stop persecuting myself about the state of Saskia's brain function. We were about to find out if my daughter had survived her ordeal intact. Soon, all would be revealed.

I didn't feel the tears running down my face in the car until a splash of water landed on my hand. Tom passed me an Enid-bright cotton hanky and I mopped myself up. Mum started a nervous chirp about God knows what from the back seat.

 'It sounds hopeful love. They wouldn't have rung else. Would they?' She needed to fill the silence.

Actually, they would. The call made no reference to a positive outcome. All we knew was Saskia had decided to wake, but her mental state hung in the balance.

As usual it was difficult to park, but on a day when it really mattered, we had a stroke of luck. Tom spotted a lady struggling to get her car out of a space and we waited patiently for her to move. Tom executed his precision parking between the white lines while Mum fumbled in her bag for parking money. We paid for three hours and decided we could feed the meter later, if needed.

Inside the hospital Mum wanted to go to the loo, so we took a detour to accommodate her. Tom and I were on tender hooks as we stood in a cream-painted corridor, waiting for her to emerge from the hospital lavatories. We took a lift to Saskia's floor where Sister greeted us.

'Fingers crossed. We've all got everything crossed for you.'

Our favourite Thai nurse was preparing the drug's trolley, and she wished us luck, too. If good wishes represented a positive outcome, we were going to be OK. But was it all about degrees of luck? A roll of the dice could be the difference between having our beautiful daughter intact or... I refused to go there again, especially when we were entering the most positive phase of our daughter's coma.

I sat Mum on a chair outside Saskia's room. She held my hand and I could see she, too, was close to tears. It was fear I remember most about that day, not relief or joy, we just shared the fear in our eyes. I was unsure what we would find in Saskia's room so it safer to leave Mum outside on a visitor's chair.

We entered to find the room full of medics and it was uncomfortably hot. Everything was beeping as usual, and I longed to open a window. Saskia's consultant caught our eye and indicated for us to return the way we'd come. Clearly Mark wanted to speak to us. He shook our hands as if it was a Rotary meeting and my mind was tumbling over itself for information.

'It is all looking good so far, but we have a way to go.'

Mark Erdington appeared calm, but I guessed he, too, was anxious. 'Saskia gave eye contact to a nurse this morning and responded to a squeeze of her hand. I believe she's on her way, but it will be slow.'

I longed for a bottle of water.

'She'll come up through various levels of consciousness and it could take some time. Hopefully, each stage will bring her closer to us.'

'What's your best guess, Mark?' It seemed the only question that mattered.

'I can only give a ballpark estimate Lottie. I know this is excruciating for you both. This is never an exact science, but I would expect her to be fully awake this evening, if all goes well.'

And if it doesn't? Did I say that out loud? No one answered so I guessed I hadn't. Mark disappeared.

I sat down next to Mum who grabbed my hand and kissed it. 'Oh Lottie. Can you believe this? Is this really happening?' She was shaking and her voice was weak. I squeezed her hand and told her we mustn't get ahead of ourselves. I'd lapsed into medical speech.

'Why don't you go in and say hello to Saskia? Tell her you're here.'

I turned to meet the eyes of a young doctor with an earnest look which would stand him in good stead when he made professor. His demeanor suggested he'd look the same in twenty years' time as he'd looked at thirteen.

'I think I'll stay here, love. You know where I am if you need me.' Mum sat down with purpose.

Tom and I entered Saskia's room with so much hope it was a physical pain. She looked exactly the same as usual, cool and beautiful, but who could see degrees of consciousness? We didn't want to get in the way of the medical staff, but they offered us seats, either side of our daughter.

'Talk to her Mrs Hanson. Like you usually do. Anything is worth trying to bring her up.'

So, we did. We kept it low-key, almost a whisper, but I told her how lovely the gardens were looking at home and I told her Blur were doing a concert in London soon. She wouldn't want to miss that. Tom said that he'd noticed Harrods had a sale and he'd take her when she woke up.

After three cups of tea on the ward and a quick trip to the hospital café, it was already seven o'clock. Tom had managed a cream tea while Mum and I toyed with Rich Tea biscuits. We heard on the TV news that John Major was running to be the new prime minister. I realised we didn't have a monopoly on problems when his grinning face poked from the television in the corner of the café. He distracted us for a few minutes. When we returned to Saskia's room we were told 'things were on schedule,' but still she hadn't woken.

After another half hour of sitting in the corridor, while doctors carried out a procedure we weren't privy to, we were called to her bedside. Saskia was awake! She had her eyes open and there was definitely life in them. I noticed the silence in her room and realised the life-support machine no longer beeped and my daughter was breathing unaided. I held her hand, unable to hold back the tears. Even Tom looked remarkably close to breaking down.

'Mum....'

The medical students and doctors left the room to give us privacy and the nurses were as discreet as they could be. 'Ssh. You're better now darling. Daddy is here too. Don't try to talk just yet.'

A nurse gave her oxygen. 'She's a good colour. You look rosy pink Saskia. Quite beautiful in fact.'

I blessed her for the comment. Nothing would please our daughter more than being told she looked beautiful.

Tom reached for Saskia's other hand, and we gazed at our daughter in disbelief. She really was awake and talking to us. Did that mean there was no brain damage? I couldn't even form the question.

We sat with her for a while and then I suggested to Tom that Mum would like to see her. It was an emotional moment. We'd all dreamed of it happening and yet it was incredibly hard to deal with. Half of me was sighing with relief and the rest of me was weeping with sadness. Staff Nurse explained Saskia would undergo various tests and it could take a couple of days for all the results to come in. So... more waiting. I was resigned to waiting and nothing could spoil that precious moment. Saskia would sleep for many hours over the coming days, the nurses informed us.

'Granny, thanks for being here.'

Mum cried unfettered tears. It was hard for us to process the moment. In my usual analytical way, I was encouraged that Saskia recognised Mum and put it in my bag of positives which was heavier than it had been for weeks.

We didn't want to leave but the nurses eventually persuaded us to go home; it was a squeak after eleven o'clock and Mum was nearly asleep on her feet.

'Saskia isn't going anywhere,' the Houseman joked. 'She'll still be here in the morning and nurses will sit with her all night. She's likely to sleep until morning. Come back after you've had some rest and you'll be ready to face tomorrow.'

He looked about sixteen and I envied him his confidence. I had so many questions but as yet, there were no answers. Would staying all night by her side have prevented something terrible happening? No, it wouldn't. Had we got a long-haul ahead of us to get Saskia fully recuperated? Yes, we had.

And so, I followed my own advice. Tom looked relieved and then I remembered he was in court the following day. I knew for certain I wouldn't be in the public gallery beside him; Saskia would come above bloody Alfie Collin's trial, of that I was sure.

We drove the dark, quiet streets in silence, yet I felt we should be celebrating. I craved a gin and tonic and it needed to be light on the tonic. I knew Tom would need at least two fingers of malt. Mum just wanted her bed.

Tom threw the house into a blaze of yellow light which made us squint. He unlocked the front door and placed the keys on the hall table before he fell into my arms. I rocked his body into mine while he sobbed into my shoulder.

'Oh Snooks. I thought she was gone forever. I never thought she'd open her eyes again.'

Mum indicated she was going to bed and disappeared upstairs.

I was staggered by Tom's outpouring. He'd never indicated his distress throughout our ordeal and behind all that outer show of coping, he was a broken man. I held him tight and tried to calm his heaving shoulders. I tried to melt love through our bodies and found I was crying too. This time it was for Tom. I cried for my selfishness in blocking him out and found it cathartic. Crying for someone you love is cleansing and somehow it took away the angst and emotion of the last few days. We had our daughter back and that was the most important thing. Any complications and all the 'what ifs,' they were for another day.

***

## Tracey

They did something called '*the summing up*' and the bun fight was close to being over. I decided to get to court early on the last day 'cos I'd spotted a place where it would be easy for Alfie to see me. I wanted to give him a smile when they took him down. I wanted him to know I was going to do everything I could to get him out.

It didn't sound like there was a cat's chance in hell that he'd get off, but at least he'd know I'd been there for him every day. That stuffed shirt from the college told the court that Alfie was given '*an opportunity boys like him would give their right arm for*'. Then he told everybody how my Alfie '*squandered what he was given*. He said my boy '*threw it back in our faces.*' I wanted to put a cowpat in his bleeding face. That's what I'd have liked to do.

I'd heard on the local jungle drums that Alfie might have been set up. Nothing stayed a secret where we lived. It sounded like another bloke was definitely involved with knifing the girl, but nothing came out in court. In a way, that made it worse 'cos how can it be cut and dried if there's doubt about who did it? Alfie told me from the beginning he never done it. I continued to zone in and out of the technical talk which mostly went over my head. I just wanted them to announce the bottom line.

Suddenly it was over. The days and days spent putting my Alfie down were over. I hoped those posh gits from the college were happy, seeing my lad go down for eight years. I stood with everybody else when the snooty cow of a judge left, but I wasn't sure my legs would carry me home.

I leaned against the stone pillar in the court lobby and tried to work out if I could reach a seat that was only a few feet away. If my knees gave way, I'd have ended up making a spectacle of myself. Deep down,

I never really expected Alfie to come home, but I kidded myself that something magical would come along and get him off.

My friend Charlene offered to come for the verdict, but I knew she'd lose money if she took time off from the factory. So I lied. I said mother was coming to court with me. Now I was on my own, fighting nausea and tears and that wasn't my way, was it? I'd never been soft.

I was still gathering courage to reach the seat when the defense brief made me jump out of my skin. I've always hated it when people creep up on me.

'I'm sorry Ms Collins, I thought we had a slim chance, but it wasn't to be.'

I thought for one awful moment he was going to put his arm around me. I sidled towards the seat. Four paces, I prayed I'd make four paces. I glared at the stuck-up prick.

'Still, never mind eh? You still get paid, don't you?

'I wouldn't say that has any relevance, Ms Collins. I'm sincerely sorry Alfie was sentenced. But we always knew it was likely, didn't we?

'We did, did we?' He didn't even speak like a normal person. 'Well, you might have been bleeding well expecting it, but I wasn't. 'It was your job to get him off.' I caught an adrenaline burst and stomped towards the door. All I wanted was to go home.

As I reached the wide stone steps of the courthouse, all hell let loose. Cameras and microphones were pushed into my face, flashlights popped, and everyone was shouting.

'Have you been to see Saskia Hanson?'

'How does it feel to know your son tried to murder a young girl?'

'Did you know Alfie took drugs?'

I looked around in desperation. My hand leapt unaided to my mouth and my eyes skittered like a frightened rabbit.

'This way. Come this way.' A man elbowed his way through the crowd towards me. I had no idea who the broad, beefy fellow was, but I followed him anyway.

'Stand aside. Let the lady though.'

'She ain't no lady,' called a wag in the crowd. 'I'm sure I put a paper bag on her head last week.'

There was a titter of appreciation for the humour. Next I found myself shoehorned into a car with its engine idling. Bulbs flashed off the windscreen and there were shouts of rage that I'd slipped the net. I knew the maggot reporters got some pictures, but I didn't care. The car lurched down Rosalind Street and took a side turning into Aldrich Way. After a couple of minutes, the driver signaled he was pulling over and he shot into a parking space.

'Who the bleeding hell are you? I spat at him like shale on a beach.

'I'm probably your saving grace and thank you wouldn't go amiss.'

'Never asked you to pick me up.'

'What did you think was going to happen to you? Nice cosy chat with the reporters over a cup of tea?'

I looked at him and for the first time noticed he'd got a taxi driver's license stuck to his dashboard. 'Listen love. You're not the first mother to see her son go down and you won't be the last. Only difference is, they usually have a few family or friends with them. Bit of a Billy-No- Mates, are you?'

'Don't need nobody. I can manage on me own. And don't think you'll get a quick blowjob out of this, 'cos you won't.'

He looked at me like I'd shocked him. He was plump with a grey beard and not much hair and was probably old enough to be my grandfather. 'Listen love. The whole world's not your enemy.'

'It bleeding well is from where I'm standing.'

'Well today it's not. OK? Now, where to? It's on me.'

He dropped me at my flat and true to his word, it was a free ride with no strings. I was glad to be home and had half an hour to myself, before I needed to collect Lily from school. I put the kettle on and sank into the sofa while it boiled. I rang Mum to tell her not to bother to fetch Lily. I told her about Alfie, too. What the hell would become of my Alfie? He'd messed up his life, big time.

I'd seen that girl's parents in court. The mother looked pale and close to tears most of the time, but the wanker of a father just looked straight ahead when he was in the dock; like he had a smell under his nose. Stuck-up pricks, both of them.

I was still asking myself if Alfie gave that girl drugs. Did he leave her to die? After everything I'd heard in court, I still didn't have an answer. I didn't want to think the worst of him. Of course I didn't. But it was hard to argue when his fingerprints were on the knife.

I could remember Alfie coming home the night of his party. It was his birthday, and he came in late. I'd heard him thumping about in his bedroom and worried he'd wake Lily. But had he just knifed a young girl? The law said he did. Mum told me no good would come of my Alfie using the art school at the college. 'He'll not fit in,' she'd said. Well, she was wrong, as usual. He seemed to have fitted in a treat.

***

*I've never done anything so exciting as being with Alfie. He's sexy Mummy. Really sexy. Even better than Jason Donovan. But you don't need to worry about me... We took everything at a slow pace. Honestly... I told him I was a virgin. I know he's not like one of us, but he'll fit in. Eventually. When you get to know him, you'll like him.*

*Alfie isn't like Dad's boys. He isn't... well educated. He talks tough and he can be mean. But he's sooo cool. He even smells exciting. I had vodka, Mum – a lot of vodka. Don't be cross with me. Alfie tried to rescue me. I think I... love him, Mum.*

## Lottie

By day two I'd started to believe Saskia was functioning fully. Little things like memories and demands for things she needed supported my belief. The effect was biblical in proportion.

On the third day I found her sitting up in bed and her nurse said she could venture into a chair that afternoon. Small steps, but they were enough to make my heart sing. She was still on a drip; the staff wanted to be sure her swallow reflex was reliable before allowing her solid food. And she was alert, although we'd been asked not to talk about the events leading to her coma. That was the difficult bit.

The registrar told us, 'There will be plenty of time for details later. And she may not remember anything about her ordeal. We prefer any kind of interaction to be done by people who are trained in these things. Try to keep conversations short and light-hearted.' He also informed us the police wanted to interview her but wouldn't be given access for a few days. I would certainly be with her for that, and it gave me something else to worry about in the middle of the night.

Poor Tom had been in court for the final few days while Mum and I spent every waking hour with Saskia. He found it stressful and struggled to communicate about the day's proceedings when he came home. Of course, I was anxious to hear of any progress, but Tom was zapped out with the trauma of it. Giving evidence was tolerable, he told me, but

193

hearing supposed intimate details about the event made him feel sick. Of course, Saskia had no idea what was happening, and it needed to stay that way until she was fully recovered.

Each day I noticed small improvements. She had physiotherapy twice a day to begin with, but her body was so weak she was unable to support her own weight. She was a shadow of our feisty daughter, but we felt blessed to have her back.

And so, it was Tom who brought Mum and me the good news that Alfie Collins was going to prison for eight years. I knew it could be reduced for good behaviour, but that did nothing to spoil the joy we felt. Justice for our daughter had been done.

Tom and I took Mum home to Cirencester where she had a warm welcome from Dad who'd missed her cooking.

'Nobody does a roast like your mother,' he said.

He was preaching to the converted. Mum started tutting about the layers of dust over the furniture and I reminded her of Dad's age and that running the farm was already a full-time job.

I pondered for a pastime. And I was sure our daughter wouldn't want anything more to do with that lad when she was fully recovered. Especially when she knew he'd been sent to prison. Surely, she'd see all his inadequacies, and she would carry the scars from the knife for the rest of her life. And then there was the matter of Saskia's pregnancy to confront.

The hospital staff talked about Saskia going home after ten days of consciousness, provided she kept all the physiotherapy appointment and continued her counselling sessions. She'd managed her first shower with support from me and I'd washed her hair in the streaming water. But she was exhausted from the effort it required and slept for most of that day. I woke her to eat but she pecked like a bird at everything I tried to tempt her with.

It was me who told her she was pregnant. The news was initially met with denial, then anger and then silence. I dangled on a piece of elastic, waiting for her to acknowledge the situation.

Eventually we took her home.

***

**Tracey**

I felt crushed and lonely. But what about my Alfie? Locked up with no hope? I had to do something. It was enough to make me get the Christmas sherry out again.

Alan popped round a couple of times but there wasn't much he could do, was there? He did get nine out of ten for his cuddles though.

Dickie told Mum he reckoned he could get Alfie off. I thought it was a bit late. He said he'd find someone to put up an alibi for him. But I knew he was all talk. You always got a lot of swanky talk from him, but I couldn't help wondering - what if for once, he was right.

And then, like a bad smell the old man let himself in through my front door. He'd got fat of late, and he rolled his body into the armchair, letting out a groan like he had a stick up his ass. I couldn't hide a look of disgust.

'Been crying, girl?'

'No. I've got a bit of hay fever is all.'

'Been to see the lad?'

'Yeh. Corse.'

'Not good in there, Trace. Still a lot of trouble on the wings.'

'Says you.'

'I know alright. I'm in the know about all sorts of things. Trust me.'

Like I'd trust the old bastard about anything, let alone my Alfie? I'd heard about the thefts and the beatings in prisons. Everybody knew about that. And I could hardly bear to think about my Alfie getting hurt. But was he having it tough?

"Pretty Boy", that's what the bastards are calling Alfie. I heard he's getting a lot of stick 'cos of his looks.'

I was dumbstruck for a minute or two. I couldn't think what to say.

'I heard he might get his head shaved. Thinks it'll make him look tougher. Sometimes the perverts wait 'til the youngsters ain't looking and then make a grab fer them in the shower.'

I was thinking what to say next. My brain had gone to mush. 'Yeh. So you said. My Alfie can look after himself.'

'Not in there he can't. Thought any more about my little proposition? Your Alfie could be safe right now if you'd agree. How hard can it be?'

I needed to buy myself some time. Time to think. I had no idea if Dickie was telling the truth, and I knew doing drug money runs was one helluva risk. 'I wanna see Alfie before I make my mind up. See if he's really in trouble. He never said anything when I saw him on Friday.'

'Well he wouldn't, would he? Go running to his mum with tales of naughty men? What do you think?'

'I still want to ask him about all this.'

'It's on your head. He's not going to tell you and the next thing, he'll be in a box. Then how will you live with yerself Trace?'

'I'll decide for myself and it won't be today.' I knew I was getting stronger at standing up to the old crook. 'Why don't you shuffle on home Dickie? Give me some peace. And leave my key on the sideboard.'

While I fetched Lily from school I couldn't stop worrying. And all Lily wanted to talk about was her brother 'cos kids at school had teased her about Alfie being in prison. It was hard. For both of us.

I'd read in the paper about that poor girl. I still couldn't get my head round my Alfie doing that to her though. Drugs maybe. He might have given her drugs. But knifing her? Never. But the court said Alfie's fingerprints were on the knife and there were witnesses who seen her at his party. His DNA was all over her, they said.

\*\*\*

## Five Years Later: Christmas 2002

### Lottie

Tom was watching a visitor's bouncing Labrador infringe our garden boundary this morning. The dog wanted to play but had no chance of a ball game with Tom, so it disappeared, leaving its slobbery ball lingering on the grass. It made me smile.

Life is good again, and the trauma of our daughter's near-death experience is fading like a bad smell. It's never quite forgotten, and I tend to pick at the scars at the least opportune moments. But we are slowly managing to leave it where it belongs, which is in the past.

The winter pansies need planting-up in the pots outside the kitchen window but I'm making chutney, so they'll have to wait. The glut of tomatoes arrived on the kitchen table this morning, courtesy of the gardener who cheerily boasted he'd, *'stripped the glasshouse bare.'* I thought they would have rotted weeks ago but I can't waste them, so here I am. The aroma has passed from yummy to throat-numbing and will probably linger for days. Olivia is 'helping' which has slowed me down, but I love having my granddaughter around. Currently, she's covered in tomato juice and looks totally adorable.

Saskia was in a stubborn mood when she first woke from her coma. However, our concerns about her brain function quickly dispersed as her intellect proved sharper than a Stanley knife. Sometimes I joked with Tom that a long sleep had made her what Dad would call '*mardy.*' Nothing we did pleased her, and anything suggested to ease her through the last trimester of her pregnancy, was met with resistance. No matter how we coaxed or cajoled, some days she barely rose from her bed, although I drew the line at room service. Enid was banned from fetching and carrying for her, too. Tom was able to appease her moods more readily than me and I waited expectantly for the return of my witty, charming daughter.

When Saskia eventually acknowledged her pregnancy, (having initially told me I was talking nonsense,) she seesawed between keeping her baby and giving it up for adoption. Although I tried to be supportive, if adoption became a reality, I had no idea how I would cope. Tom, of course, was all for it. He felt his wishes had been ignored over the abortion issue and blatantly encouraged our daughter to give up her baby and get on with her life. I searched for the old Saskia in the shadow of the new one, but some days the view was misted. It was a slow process, but at least we had something to encourage and sustain us daily.

Saskia still hankered after a medical career, so she caught up with her exams at the local community college.  She wasn't brave enough to continue at Churchill's, and who could blame her?  But there was a part of me, a mischievous particle of my previous self, that envisaged a pregnant Saskia in a Churchill's classroom. I suspected there'd be a scattering of apoplectic figures at risk of heart failure.

We knew Saskia was bright enough to pick up her studies and had no concerns about her making it into medical school. I admired her pluck; she was very obviously pregnant but showed no embarrassment among her fellow students.

I told myself Saskia and I bonded while we drove to pre-natal classes once a week and I glimpsed her old self beneath the grumpy moods and withdrawal from family life.  I usually booked a table for lunch so that the classes became more of an occasion, and I saw signs we were getting our loving daughter back. Sometimes she mentioned Alfie and I had to accept that if she kept the baby, he would be given access.

 'I want her to know who her dad is. It's important. Being an adopted child, it's something I'll never know.'

It was gut-wrenching to know our daughter pined for something I couldn't give her, and I worried it would blight her life. I talked to her about the possibility of Tom and me taking responsibility for the baby when it arrived. I told her we could keep it until she was ready to be a mother. I even suggested she might like a trip to Cornwall after the baby was born as I thought some time apart from us would help her make the right decision about her child.

And then two milestones arrived at once. Our granddaughter made her entrance into the world and Tom gave his notice to Churchill's College. He'd decided, without any reference to me, that we would move to the family pile near Oxford. I guessed that Tom felt unable to carry out his work at Churchill's after the court case, and I could understand that. But given the opportunity, I'd have been a good listener and helped him simulate his thought processes

By the time he shared his plans with me he'd already given his cousin notice and was making arrangements for our new life. I was totally unprepared, and it was nothing short of earth-shifting.

And so, the Hansons and the Collins were destined to mingle over the crib of our granddaughter Olivia. Alfie professed to love Saskia while, thankfully, she was more guarded about her feelings. But I was pleased she'd cared enough to ensure all his convictions were dropped.

Although the Appeal Hearing had been gruelling. Saskia and I had spent long hours in the police station, many of them sitting in grubby corridors next to a variety of dubious characters. I supported my daughter while she had to relive the horror of that night. When the police officer noted Saskia was pregnant, she asked if there was to be an allegation of rape. There wasn't. Eventually the law was satisfied that Alfie Collins was innocent of the crimes and agreed to his release.

Upon release he door-stepped our house for days. He'd heard Saskia was home from hospital and pregnant, and eventually we had to let him see her. I insisted there would be no bedroom visits, so Saskia dressed and put on makeup before he was allowed in.

Tom had to deal with the logistics of Alfie's first visit, as it was beyond my ability to welcome that scoundrel into our home. But invade my private space he did, and when he left, I felt as violated as if we'd had a burglar in our home. However, it became obvious Alfie would continue to demand his right to see his child when she was born, so eventually I managed to nod an acceptance when he was in my home.

While the weather stayed fine Saskia and Alfie's meetings were in the garden, out of our earshot. I imagined they planned and schemed, who knew what? I was paranoid about his ability to influence my daughter and scared witless the relationship would linger. I think Tom worried Alfie would waylay Saskia's desire to take up medicine. But over the weeks I noticed a gradual loss of interest from her. A couple of times when Alfie came to see her, she sent him away saying she was unwell. I revelled in those moments.

In time we had to face the fact that Alfie Collins would have access to his daughter. Saskia would not budge on the issue, so we tried to accept it. Any argument we put forward was ignored. I tried to hide my irritation with my daughter and constantly reminded myself how close we'd come to losing her. But it wasn't easy. The sleepless nights continued, and it seemed my head had no respite from worry now the goal posts had moved.

It was me who took a wriggling Olivia Charlotte into my arms when she was born, and we've loved her every day since her arrival. I did the night feeds and the nappy changing and I took her to the clinic to be weighed and vaccinated. She felt as though she was mine although I was mindful that she was on loan. Saskia took the odd look into the pram and was grumpy if woken at night by her crying infant.

After keeping me on edge for weeks, Saskia finally agreed that Tom and I could bring up her daughter while she got her life back on track. However, she insisted Alfie would continue his access visits.

The minefield that was Alfie Collins was ever present and impossible to eradicate, and I could see he was in our lives for the long haul. But although I hated him near our granddaughter, the legal decision was not in my hands. I fully agreed the lad shouldn't linger in prison if, indeed, he hadn't wielded the knife nor pumped my daughter full of drugs, but I needed to distance him from our lives. Being a realist, I knew that wasn't to be.

Tom had never mentioned encountering problems at work as a direct result of Saskia's behaviour, although it was inevitable they'd had an impact on his life at Churchill's. I guess I was so wrapped up in my own worries that I didn't care about anything else. I had occasionally wondered if his job would survive, especially when the gruesome details about sex and drugs were made common knowledge at the trial, but it felt trivial compared to having a daughter in a drug-fuelled coma.

With hindsight, I don't believe Tom was pushed from his position of House Master, but he probably felt alone while making major decisions about both his career and the wellbeing of his family. Which, I suppose makes me an insensitive bitch. But I paid the price because the move to the family seat got under way early in the Michaelmas term, whether I liked it or not.

'It will be a great place to bring up Olivia,' Tom persuaded me. 'And I'll make sure my mother doesn't interfere. I promise.' I was less than sure about that.

Things moved quickly and before Olivia's first birthday we were settled in the baronial home with the mother–in-law –from- hell still ensconced in the Dower House on the edge of the estate. Saying goodbye to Churchill's was harder than I'd expected, especially as we were inundated with gifts from all quarters. Boys arrived at our apartment with sentimental cards and presents and the school gave us a stunning antique chest which we'll cherish. From the staff, we had a framed water colour of our house which encompasses the beautiful garden over which I'd pondered for so many hours while Saskia lay sleeping. I felt deeply humbled by the outpouring of love for our family and it made it hard to move on with our lives.

My friend Heidi told me to 'buck up' when she found me in tears at the kitchen table the day before the move. She reminded me I was about to embark upon an exciting challenge, and I was a 'lucky bunny' to be inheriting a Cotswold pile and a title. She practiced a curtsy and said she was damned if she was going to call me 'Ma'am. Of course, she made me laugh and we made promises to stay in touch.

Dear Enid was another matter. She was unable to hide her dismay at our departure and at one point I thought Tom might offer her a cottage on the estate. But we left with our little family intact, and I wallowed in the joy of having Saskia back where she belonged.

When we tipped up at Knoxbury Hall I was still in aftershock from the unexpected changes to our lives. Olivia had just started crawling, so she was all over the place and certainly had no intention of being contained for more than an hour or two. Consequently, I had little input to the packing or unpacking of our belongings. It was a slightly surreal experience. We wanted to be in the Hall before Christmas and the operation was completed in less than a week. *'Put the crystal in the glass cabinet. No, the other glass cabinet.'*

I may not have made a physical contribution to the move, but my throat was raw from calling instructions. Unusually, our new home was already stuffed with antique furniture so we had to juxtaposition our own where we could. I had always thought our living space was generous at Churchill's, but this was gargantuan by comparison. Mum and Dad came up for a few hours to help, but we happily left the donkey work to the professionals. It was, however, lovely to have them share Olivia's boisterous energy.

Tom announced he had plans to open the house to the public to pay for its upkeep. Around two hundred acres had been rented out by Tom's brother years before, but the income came nowhere near what was required. There was a herd of one hundred Devon Red cattle on the other hundred acres and an enclosure of angora sheep. Apparently, we were going to convert a barn into a tearoom and make ice cream in the old dairy. We might find someone to spin the angora wool into saleable skeins, I offered. Tom had decided we'd employ local people to get his ideas off the ground and I would have the luxury of part-time childcare for Olivia. Things skipped along, mostly according to plan.

\*\*\*

## Tracey

I heard when that girl woke up and I was as pleased for her family as anyone else; I was even more pleased when they released my Alfie. I was full of guilt too for not believing he was innocent, but I had to put all that behind me when the real shock came. My Alfie announced I was going to be a grandmother. He was like a dog with two tails, but I could see beyond the first flush of excitement, and I worried how it would work out. I didn't want him hurt, although he assured me his name was on the birth certificate.

What with the trauma of Alfie going down and then the death of Old Dickie, I'd had a lot to deal with. The old bugger lived just long enough to see Alfie released from prison. I wasn't sure how I felt, if I'm honest. It must have been a terrible death, being burnt alive, and I wouldn't wish that on anyone. I don't think there was much of him left to put in a coffin. My Lily cried 'cos she liked the old sod. But me, it was a different matter for me 'cos he was answerable for a lot that was wrong with my life. But I eventually came to realise what he was, and I wouldn't be remembering him as a kind old man who took pity on a struggling single Mum, either.

When the court released Alfie, it made Lily and me unbelievable happy. And even better, Alfie was released before I had to get mixed up with collecting money on the DODO run. That would surely have got me into real trouble with the law.

A week or so after Dickie's funeral, a solicitor rang Alfie and asked him to call in to his office with his passport. I panicked as I was afraid there was a technical hitch with his release papers from the court, although Alfie was sure it wasn't that. I had to keep myself busy when he went 'cos I wasn't up for any more bad news. I'd had my fair share of troubles and probably my mother's share as well. I spent a couple of hours spring cleaning the house, but I couldn't put my mind to it.

And then Alfie came back from town grinning from ear to ear. He rushed through the door and picked me off my feet and swung me around like a windmill. I screamed with delight knowing that whatever it was, it wasn't bad news.

'Guess what?' he asked. Well, I couldn't guess. How could I? Eventually I got the news out of him but not before he dashed to the corner shop and came back with four cans of lager, and a bottle of white wine for me. I knew this had to be something special.

Alfie told me he could remember taking a large brown envelope from Dickie to the solicitors, not long before the fire at Dickie's flat. He said he thought about steaming it open but couldn't be bothered. He was thinking it might have been Dickie's will, and it turned out it was, and he'd left everything to my Alfie. Alfie was so excited that I joined in his happiness – it was impossible not to. But actually, I never thought Dickie had much. He'd been living off the Social ever since he was beaten up on his way home from the pub one night. It was such a brutal attack that his legs never worked again, and it seemed to age him overnight; all the fight went out of him. I called on him now and then, but Alfie told me I was a fool 'cos he'd ruined my life. I thought that anything Dickie had to leave Alfie would have burnt in his flat.

But it turned out I was wrong. Dickie had shares and gold bars stashed away worth somewhere around three hundred thousand pounds in all. Alleluia! That was something to get my head round, wasn't it? Lady Luck had found out where we lived at last.

We're only allowed to see Alfie's daughter twice a month and I always try to make it special. Livi loves my Lily who's very sweet with her. She'd change her nappies and feed her when she was little, and she'd even clear up her muddles. She was a little mother to her. Now Livi's bigger Alfie takes them both to the zoo and sometimes to the indoor pool. I always push the boat out for a nice tea and Alfie's little girl seems to fit in with us a treat.

One year, Alfie asked if he could take Livi on holiday, but the snooty mother said no. She said they were off to Cornwall. We don't get much of a look in, but we make the best of it. I can see that having Olivia in his life is making Alfie try to turn his life around.

It was a lot of money that plopped into Alfie's account after all the paperwork was done on Old Dickie's estate. Although my son claimed it was dirty money, I could see a way it could change our lives forever. Alfie had taken himself off to college after his release from prison where he completed a motor mechanics course he'd started while he was inside. Alan helped him get a job when he finished his training, and I was so proud of him. The job was poorly paid compared to dealing drugs, but Alfie swore all that was behind him because he had Livi to consider.

I did a bit of digging around the estate agents and found a perfect little car business for sale on the outskirts of Oxford. It wasn't far from where the posh ones had taken his daughter to live and there was a small flat above the garage workshop, big enough for Alfie and his daughter when she came to stay. Not that she's been allowed to stay with us so far, but Alfie intends to go to court to get better access. If Alfie bought the business, I thought I'd swap my housing association flat for something nearer to him. I was buzzing with excitement, which was rather an unusual feeling, and I liked it.

Alan was still on the scene. We dated all through the first year Alfie came home. Lily loves him and we often go to his house for the weekend. But when he asked me to marry him I was scared shitless. I said no because I had no idea how to say yes. But we've stayed friends, and he is the nicest bloke I've ever known. I hope he asks me to marry him again 'cos I think I'd say yes if he did. I don't think he's bothered with other girls, so there's hope.

After a lot of nagging Alfie arranged to look at the garage. And he thought it looked OK. I thought it was brilliant but tried to keep my excitement under wraps. I knew Alfie would take some persuading to make the move, but I was thinking it would get him away from all his druggy mates and nearer to his daughter. Lily said she wouldn't mind moving school as long as it was soon 'cos she was getting close to secondary school age. She also liked the idea of going to a new school where nobody knew her brother had been in prison. Of course, it would be good for me to leave a load of baggage behind, too.

Moving away from Alan was the only thing that was not so good, but when I told him about it he said fifteen miles was nothing and we'd still keep seeing each other. He was excited for me and the kids and encouraged me to push Alfie into buying his own business.

You should have seen the estate agent's face when Alfie told her it was a cash sale. I felt like I was Princess Diana and I'd never been so happy in my life. It looked as though I was going to be a proper person at last, the sort of person who lives a decent life and can be a good mother. I think I'm getting' there.

I've hardly dared get used to being a grandma yet, in case the snooty ones on the estate take her away. Money always counts doesn't it, but we all enjoy having little Livi when we can.

Lily loves her new school, and I think she'll do well in her exams. She wants to be a nurse and that makes me dead proud. I'll do anything to help her get there. We were so lucky to get a flat swap to Oxford and it's a better home than we left behind. Lily has a proper sized bedroom, and the living room is much bigger.

I've found a job in a local factory making motorbike seats. I discovered I was a quick learner and I'm getting good bonuses for the speed and quality of my work. The money is just enough to go round, and I've got a little nest egg which Alfie gave me from Dickie's money. I'm keeping it safe so that Lily can go to university.

'I'll pay my own way Mum.' Lily said when I told her. 'Just spend it on yourself.'

As if I'll do that.


I'm so proud of my Alfie; nobody would recognise him these days. He's even got a lad working for him on an apprentice scheme. He's got more work than he can handle and puts in long hours to get everything done. It helps that he lives above the garage, but I think he's eating a lot of takeaway food which isn't good for him.

We both worried about who would do his books when he bought the business, 'cos neither of us has a clue about accounts. Luckily, the lady who'd done it for the previous owner was happy to stay on, so Alfie can get stuck into the cars that keep arriving for repair. He's talking about being an MOT centre in a couple of years.

I'm still waiting for something to spoil our new lives 'cos we're not known for being lucky.

***

*Mummy – you are going to find this hard and you'll think me a heartless bitch but... the thing is... I don't want Olivia. I don't want to be a mother... I want freedom to start a new life without her. I think it's time she was adopted, don't you?*

## Lottie

We are preparing for our fourth Christmas in Knoxbury Hall and Saskia is coming home. The roast is sizzling in the oven and lunch is well under way. I've chosen pork because it's Saskia's favourite and I know she rarely gets the chance to indulge. I remember my student days when pasta with sauce was my staple diet, and nothing suggests that it has changed.

'Granny, can I have some bird seeds?'

'We fed them this morning,' I remind Olivia.

'Yes, but the magpies ate most of it and the robin is looking really hungry. He's on the wall and I think he's waiting to be fed.' Olivia's face falls and I can't resist her plea.

'OK, but you'll have to come and get it 'cos I'm busy cooking lunch for Mummy.'

'Only Mummy?' Can we all have some?'

I rustle her dark curls and notice the red highlights which are her only genetic nod to her mother. Without doubt she's Alfie's; he's passed on his soft brown skin and melting toffee eyes.

'Yes, we'll all have some,' I reply. 'Even Nathan likes roast pork.' I watch her eyes at the mention of Nate, but she gives little away.

'Does Daddy like pork?'

'Probably. I think everyone likes it. Can you manage the lid on the birdseed?'

'I'm four, Granny. Have you forgotten?'

I bend to kiss my precious granddaughter and ask her not to be over-generous with the bird seed. She has a tendency to throw the lot at them when the weather is as cold as today and claims they're all starving. But what's a bit of bird seed in the greater scheme of things? Papa will help if you ask him,' I say.

'I can manage. I can do it.'

Of course she can. Ever since she crawled at eight months old, she's been independent and now she's at school, she's romping away at an alarming rate.

I'm so looking forward to seeing Saskia. After she came through the coma unscathed, I believed she was our own special miracle. And although I'm not a believer in a greater being, I accept we were blessed with her recovery and try to remember it every day of my life. I'll never forget the very dark days, the days when I was at breaking point; Tom and I were both imagining the worst but praying for the best and those prayers were answered. These days, it's hard to spoil Saskia as we see her so seldom. When she chose to do her medical training in Exeter, it was inevitable she wouldn't get home too often, but she's coming home for Christmas. We're having two

Christmas trees this year and they're in the stable block waiting for Saskia and Olivia to magic them into glowing, shimmering works of art.

I can hear the phone ringing and wipe my hands clean from peeling potatoes.

'Hi Mum. We're running about half an hour late. Sorry. Traffic's bad. We'll be another hour.'

'No probs Darling. I'll hold lunch. I haven't put the roasties in yet. '

'Mmm... I can smell them already. I'll get Nate to drive faster.'

'Safer. Tell him to drive safer. That's all that matters.'

'I know, I know. Just teasing. See you soon.'

I go outside to tell Olivia that her Mummy and Nate will be arriving in a while, but she's totally engrossed in birdseed.

'Okay. Granny, do you think the magpies will eat all these seeds before the robin gets a chance? Shall I stand here and guard the bird table?'

I laugh. 'No Olivia, you can't do that Darling. You'll frighten all the birds away if you stay outside.'

She frowns and is probably learning that life isn't always fair. 'Can Daddy come for lunch?'

'Not today. You're seeing Daddy on Boxing Day, remember?'

'Oh yes. And Lily. She told me she's going to have real makeup for Christmas. Do you believe her?'

'If she says so,' I say. 'She doesn't usually tell lies.'

'How does Father Christmas know about girl's makeup? He's a man.'

'Well, some men know a lot about makeup, or maybe some of the elves are girls. That would work.'

'Mmm, I never thought about that.'

We hurry indoors before the biting wind seeps up trouser legs and nibbles at delicate skin. I put on my festive CD and revel in the joy of the Eton Boys singing carols while peeling the potatoes. I remind Olivia the Snowman film is on the TV, but she declines in favour of her Lego.

I can hear Tom in the shower and he's cutting it a bit fine 'cos the kids will arrive any minute. I've managed a quick stroke of lipstick and brushed my hair, but all the hallmarks of a busy cook are apparent on my face. I've held back lunch so that we can all have a drink when they arrive.

We don't know Nate very well, but we're pleased he's joining us for Christmas. Tom and I approve of him, so it'll probably be a short-lived relationship. Saskia has had some gruesome fellas over the last few years and Alfie is included in the number. However, I take each day as it comes, as Mum would say. All Tom and I want for Saskia is to see her graduate and find a job that makes her happy.

I'm determined this Christmas will be perfect. I only have one shot at it as I think Saskia and Nathan are spending Boxing Day with his parents and the New Year in London with friends. London will undoubtedly be a more spirited venue than life in the Hanson household. Mum and Dad will make it for Christmas lunch, but they'll need to get back for the milking. I've noticed they're starting to show their age and dared to suggest they might consider retirement a few weeks ago. I'd like to see them take things easy for a few years. Dad will need some persuading to give up the farm which represents his lifetime's work, although I think Mum can see the advantages of not having their lives ruled by the needs of the livestock. Tom suggested they may like to settle on the estate, but that is all for discussion after Christmas.

I can hear a car and call Olivia away from her Lego creation.

'Do you think Mummy will like it? A frown of concentration ruckles her face.

'I'm sure she will. Quick. They're here.'

There's a bundle of cuddles and hellos in the hallway and everyone is shining with the glow of Christmas. Saskia lifts her daughter sky-high and makes her scream with laughter.

'I'm nearly five, Mummy. I'm not a baby.' When she arrives at floor level, she wraps her arms around her mother's hips and hugs her. 'I've missed you Mummy. You haven't even seen my Lego'.

'In a while. Let me get inside, baby.'

'It's huge and I did it all myself. She catches Tom's eye, 'well most of it. Papa helped a bit, didn't you Papa?

'I did, but most of the work was done by you.' Tom is generous to a fault where his granddaughter is concerned.

I edge everyone into the sitting room before they congregate in the kitchen and Tom is already taking orders for drinks. Nate has gone to bring in their luggage from the car and I give Saskia another hug. It's great to have her home, even if I must share her these days.

'Look Mummy. Look. Do you like it?'

Saskia bends to take the Lego from her daughter's hand. 'I love it Poppet. You are a clever girl. Maybe you'll be a doctor like Mummy, when you're older.'

'Do you make people better?'

'Not yet, but in a couple of years' time I shall. Nate will be making people better next year. How cool is that?'

Olivia is unimpressed and I'm slightly edgy. I know my daughter well and I'm picking up a vibe I can't analyse. She's slightly spikey and I'm wondering why. But I leave them to it and return to the kitchen to make the gravy.

'Do you want your usual, darling?' Tom calls.

'Please. Not too strong.'

Saskia joins me. 'Olivia is really into her Lego, isn't she? Clever little sausage.'

'She loves building things.' A wash of sadness reminds me how little Saskia knows about her daughter. Sometimes it feels as if she's her tiresome kid sister who has a tendency to get in her way.

Tom brings me a gin and tonic flushed with ice. 'I've left yours in the sitting room Saskia. Shall I bring it?'

'I expect Olivia wants to show you all her princess drawings,' I interrupt. 'She's got a drawer of them waiting to show Mummy.' I know I sound pushy. However much I want Saskia to want to spend time with her daughter, I see little sign of it.

'No thanks, Dad. I'll go and find Nate.'

I avoid Tom's eyes and concentrate on getting food to the table while it's piping hot.

Lunch is a success. The roast is much admired and large appetites are sated. Except Olivia, who allows her mother to cut her pork, appeases her by spooning broccoli onto her plate, but eats little. She pushes her lunch around the plate until it resembles soup and rarely takes her eyes off Nate. It's hardly surprising she feels jealous of her mother's latest boyfriend.

Saskia and Nate want to pop into town after lunch to finish their Christmas shopping. Olivia is not invited.

'I have no idea what to buy the man who has everything. Any ideas for Dad?' Saskia asks while I scrape plates.

We have this conversation every year and each Christmas it gets harder. The truth is, he'd be happy with a box of fudge from Sennen, but that feels an inadequate gift for a father for Christmas. 'Why don't you get him a jumper from M&S?' I hear myself suggesting the default item which can never be called exciting, by any stretch of the imagination.

'I'm sure I'll find something.' She swings her pine-green, hand-knitted scarf around her auburn hair and kisses my cheek. A whirl of winter leaves rush the hallway as they disappear.

'I didn't want to go. If Mummy had asked me, I didn't want to go.'

I feel a squeeze on my heartstrings. 'I need you here, darling. We have to wrap Mummy's present, and you can do your best writing on her card. She'll be so surprised how well you can write, won't she?'

'Have we got a present for Nate?'

'We have. Just something small. Would you like to see what it is?'

We climb the stairs to the guest room which has a duffel bag and two carrier bags of stuff dumped on the floor. I peek inside Saskia's room and it looks like a Medina. They're sleeping together, of course. After all the shenanigans when Saskia was sixteen, it seems useless to be prissy about their sleeping arrangements now.

'Is Daddy's present in here? I need to wrap it and write a card for him, too. Did we buy Lily anything?'

I sigh. It doesn't get any easier. Well, maybe just a little. At least I can look Alfie Collins in the eye and know he didn't bestow permanent damage on our daughter. But I need more than that, these days. I want my granddaughter to have a more settled life. I don't want her to be the odd one out, the one without her mother around, the one who drifts between us and her father. Tom tells me *'blended families'* are the norm these days, but I see Olivia as part of a fragmented family. And I wanted so much more for her. It seems the longer she and her mother live apart, the cooler their relationship becomes. No surprises there.

When Olivia was born, I knew the spark between Saskia and Alfie was already extinguished. Saskia was tired of him, as I predicted, although I knew Alfie felt differently about her. So why, I asked myself, did he have to have access to our granddaughter. It would have been different if they were together; then I'd have had to get used to the yob visiting our home. But Saskia was belligerent, and it was not up for discussion.

I had no conscience about fighting with every dirty trick I knew to persuade our daughter to change her mind. I felt a clean break was the easier option, certainly for Tom and me who would be bringing Olivia up for the foreseeable future. But Saskia would not be moved. Alfie Collins would have access to his daughter, and I had to make some kind of deal with my anger. I'd got my daughter back, so it had to be give-and-take, I reasoned. I'd made deals with God after all, so this was probably pay-back time. Tom took the moral high ground with an unspoken '*told you so.*'

But the aggravation didn't stop with Alfie Collins because Tracey claimed her rights as a grandmother, too. And it was at this point, I realised Churchill's

College had turned me into a snob. For whatever reason, I didn't want my precious grandchild to be tarnished by the likes of that family. Apparently, Olivia was shown to them as a small baby on one of Alfie's access visits and there'd been regular contact since. I'm told they were both welcomed into Tracey's home, 'like part of the family.' Saskia told me, 'The house is spotless Mum. And they really love Olivia.' Hmm... I hated the world at that moment and made no more deals with God.

Saskia and Nate return with arms full of presents and Olivia's excitement is palpable.

'Are they for me Mummy? Are they all for me?'

'No, you little minx. Father Christmas brings your presents, doesn't he?'

'Only some. You have to buy me some too. Have you forgotten?' Her little face crumples. Suddenly the flood-gates open and she sobs into my skirt. 'Granny said some presents come from Father Christmas and some from Mummy and Daddy.' I receive a dark look from under her eyelashes which called me a liar. 'Do you think Daddy has forgotten me, too?'

I meet Saskia's eyes and see her fear. She has no idea how to handle her daughter.

'Darling, in some families it's Granny and Papa who buy presents. That's what happens when Mummies are busy.'

'Are you sure?' Her little chin is still wobbling.

'Quite sure and I don't want any peeping when I wrap them up. Do you promise?'

She gives me a hug. 'You're the best, Granny. And Papa.' She turns to Tom, 'Did you buy me a present too?'

'I did, angel. You can be sure your pile of presents will be mountain high.' He raises his arms to the heavens and placates her. My darling grandchild immediately brightens. She smiles and gives Tom a limpet hug. 'Thank you, Papa. Thank you.'

Saskia helps me wrap Olivia's presents on Christmas Eve. It's lovely to have my daughter to myself and I ask her about uni. It's a safe subject. I try not to be too inquisitive about her life, but after nursing her back to health, I find it impossible to forget her lack of judgement on that fateful night. Tom and I think Nate is a steady influence and hope the relationship survives Christmas and New Year. Don't they say stress levels at this time of year can impact on couples? I think Nate will be doing something without Saskia after New Year so, hopefully, we shall have our daughter back and all to ourselves for a few days, which is just as well as I know something is brewing. I can't pinpoint the issue, and I don't think it's between Saskia and Nate, so it's either her training or her daughter. I just pray she isn't pregnant.

### Tracey

My Alfie still loves that girl. I've told him to get out and find a new one, but he says all his time and effort is going into his business and his daughter. He's doing dead good at both. He's built the business up and I'm real proud of him.

It's been a bit of a long haul these last few years. I don't think I'll ever get over the stress of those months after Alfie was arrested. They've left permanent scars on me. And then there was Dickie's death. Silly old sod left a ciggy burning and it caught the chair alight. They didn't get him out in time and as his legs were already knackered, he must have burned to a crisp. My Alfie said it was no more than he deserved, but I wouldn't go that far. Funny thing was, it turned out Dickie had all that money and gold hidden away. Who'd have thought that?

Ever since he got out, Alfie's stayed clean 'cos his daughter means everything to him. Looks like he's turned his life around. In fact, we all have. And Old Dickie's money was a Godsend, even though Alfie called it dirty money. But I told him it was the only chance he was likely to get to make something of his life and who cared what colour the money was? For once he listened to me.

Livi is coming to our house on Boxing Day. Well, actually it's to Alfie's flat, but Lily and me will be there when she arrives. I can't wait. We'll have another Christmas Day just for my granddaughter and Lily has hidden little gifts for her in the Christmas tree. Hope the whole bleeding lot don't come down while she's looking.

I can hardly believe our good news. We've never had much good luck in our family, but it's dropped like hailstones today. That snooty girl, I suppose now I shall have to pretend I like her 'cos of what she's done, is letting my Alfie have full custody of his daughter. I can't get my head around it, but he's already said Lily and me can have his flat and he's looking for a house with a mortgage for him and Livi to live in. I told him it needs to be close to the business so that I can help with Livi. It's been a real pinch-me couple of days.

I shan't give notice on the flat we're in at the moment 'cos I think it will take a while to sort the legal stuff. But I can't believe Lily and me will be living in my Alfie's property. It's the first time we haven't been in social housing for the whole of our lives and it's gonna be great.

I don't want Lily to have to change school again 'cos she's doing so well. She needs to stay where she is until she's done her GCSE's. If she wants to be a nurse, she'll need to stay on for A levels but all that is something for the future. I can't get used to the warm feeling I've got in my stomach. I worry that somebody will take it away from me.

Alan and me are still an item. I wish I was brave enough to tell him I'd like to marry him now.

***

*Mummy... this is going to be tough but... Alfie wants to have care and custody of Olivia and... I've told him he can have her. The thing is, he's her father and although you've been wonderful, I think it best if she goes to Alfie. He's her blood relation and... I know how it feels to have no blood relations. Sorry if I'm causing you and Daddy pain. I thought maybe you would like to keep Olivia until after her birthday while Alfie deals with the custody papers. If it makes it easier, I'll come up from Exeter to take her to Alfie, when the time comes.*

### Lottie

Our fourth Christmas at Knoxbury Hall was a joy and while Olivia slowly warmed to Nate, her relationship with Saskia dropped into a familiar rhythm. We trod the usual road of over-indulgence, silly hats and inane television and by Christmas night we were all exhausted. I confessed to being relieved that Saskia and Nate were going to his parents the following day, but I stressed about Olivia spending Boxing Day with Alfie. Something still curdled in my stomach at the mention of his name.

When Saskia put Olivia to bed, I heard her say she and Nate were leaving in the morning and they would take her to Daddy's around ten o'clock. That meant either Alfie would return her to us, or we'd have to fetch her. Neither was an easy option.

Boxing Day breakfast was a quiet affair consisting predominately of coffee. Olivia suggested we share the left-over trifle but was soon dissuaded when she found an unopened present in the dining room.

'See you in a few days.' Saskia, Nate and Olivia waved from the car and with a crunch of gravel they were gone.

'I really must get John to sweep these paths.'

My husband noticed imperfections that I passed off as normal life. Tom was never off duty now we had the estate to care for. I was thinking the bloody leaves could wait, and anyway, who could expect staff to work on Boxing Day? For me the dampener was Alfie Collins who would bring our granddaughter back in a few hours.

As usual after a family Christmas, the analysis followed.

'Great food, Snooks. You really pushed the boat out and you deserve a few days of peace and quiet.'

'Wasn't it lovely to have her home? Don't you think she seems more grounded since she's been with Nate?'

'If I was a betting man, I'd say he's the one. Their relationship feels close to me. But I'm only a man, so I could be wrong!'

'Well I hope you're right, on this occasion.'

'They could have a great life together.'

'Did you get the feeling Saskia wants to talk to us about something? Did you pick up a slightly... I don't know what, but I think something is afoot.'

'Can't say I did. She seemed perfectly normal to me.'

I can sense the game is changing and my heart tells me we'll soon be major players in our granddaughter's life. I can't see how Olivia is ever going to fit with her mother's ambitions. Nate was sweet with her but it's a big ask of any fellow to take on another man's child. And I can't help thinking about the long hours they will have to work in hospital.

Tom loves his granddaughter in a way that is heaven to watch. He taught her to read and can't resist getting in the pool and encouraging her to shed the water wings. She's brought out a softer side in him. If I ponder the abortion issue, which I sometimes do, I remember the tenacity with which I nurtured that baby in Saskia's womb. I'm sure Tom is pleased it was an argument he lost.

On Boxing Day evening, it was me who opened the door to Alfie Collins and Olivia and I could see she was hyped on sugar.

'Granny, I want to show Daddy my presents from Father Christmas.'

What could I do? I opened the door wide enough for him to come in and left Olivia to show him to her room.

'Well done Snooks. He doesn't bite, does he?' Tom handed me a large gin and tonic.

'He didn't, but he looks as if he might.'

'Come on love. It's been nearly five years, and he is her father.'

'I know and I feel guilty. Maybe we should offer him a drink. It is Christmas.'

'Hell must have frozen over, Lottie. Okay. I'll catch him as he comes downstairs with Olivia. It'll please her, for sure.'

It was probably the hardest half hour since Saskia's coma. Alfie accepted our invitation to have a beer and followed Tom into the drawing room. I think a nod was forthcoming from me, but I can't be sure.

'I've had a great day with Livi. She played with my kid sister, and we took her to feed the ducks. I wrapped her up warm.' He looked at me. 'Mum loves to see her.'

There was one of those awkward silences I'd learned to deal with all those years ago. I just looked back at Alfie Collins who, if anything, was even better looking than when I saw him in court. Except for his grimy fingernails which were probably achieved courtesy of his mechanic's job. I'd heard on the grape vine he was doing well with his business and who could begrudge him that?

'She's got a load of presents in the car. Shall I get them?'

He looked as if a quick escape would be a blessing. But I heard myself say, 'why don't you finish your beer first. Did you have a good Christmas?'

He pinned me with those chocolate eyes and for the first time I could see how he attracted Saskia. His daughter stayed close to his side, and he ruffled her hair and stroked her cheek as he talked.

'Yeh, it was great. Mum's not much of a cook but we had a turkey ready by five o'clock. I gave her a microwave for Christmas, but she hasn't worked out how to use it yet.'

'Business good is it? Tom sounded as if he was really interested, an attribute which comes as standard if Churchill's is in your bloodline.

'Doing great, thanks. Month by month the turnover's rising... I'm doing a simple bookkeeping course at Tech.'

'Ah, commendable.'

With that Alfie gulped his beer and placed the glass on a table. 'Thanks for that.' He picked up his daughter and kissed her. I've got to go now, Rascal. But I'll see you soon, okay?'

Olivia started to cry.

'Don't cry, poppet. Come with Daddy to get your presents out of the car. You can show Granny and Grandpa.'

'You mean Papa. He's called Papa.'

'Exacting little miss, ain't you?'

I could feel the chill in the hall as he left the door ajar. He gave Olivia a shopping bag from Asda which was full of her gifts, and I heard him tell her to hurry indoors before she got cold.

And then he was gone. I looked at Tom for a reaction, but he was inscrutable.

During the midweek lull between Christmas and New Year, that annual slump when everyone has over-indulged, I can think of nothing but adopting Olivia. It makes perfect sense, and I know Tom will be okay with it, too. But he keeps telling me not to jump the gun as Saskia has yet to put the idea to us. But I know she will, and I can barely contain my excitement. I have a million plans in my head, just waiting to be put into practice when I'm a Mum again. What a precious gift she'll be.

Saskia is coming home after New Year for a few days before she returns to uni so it will be the perfect time to set things in motion. I can see several positives around the logistics, not least, that Olivia won't need to change her surname. Hanson is on her birth certificate, well I haven't seen it, but Saskia told me so. And she'll be a Hanson until she marries.

The most important point is not the legal process or how Tom and I feel, it has to be about Olivia and how she might adapt to the new arrangements. Will Olivia feel rejected by her mother? Only time will tell. And I can't think about Alfie Collins having access to his daughter as that will mar my excitement and God knows, I deserve a little bit of good luck to go my way.

Over the last five years I've carved a niche for myself on the estate, despite having little input into Tom's initial ideas. He spent more time than I thought was healthy consulting his mother when we first moved. And he continues to visit her each day for his afternoon tea. I don't receive an invite thank God, and Olivia avoids her like the plague.

But the time Tom spent with his mother paid dividends because she grudgingly agreed to the proposed changes necessary to open to the public. There was a proviso, however, that the public were not to stray within twenty metres of her house. I could understand her concerns about members of the public tramping all over her senior years, but Tom ensured she was happy when we drew his ideas on large sheets of paper. We wanted to put a one-way system in place so that visitors would enter and exit through the main gates where a huge car parking area was created from one of the meadows. The planners were amazingly receptive to our ideas, so there were few delays with starting the new business.

The Grand Dame made one effort to welcome us to the Dower House which morphed into the teatime from hell. Olivia was about ten months old and wound up with excitement; she refused to sit still, no matter how much I coaxed. The little monkey threw the proffered biscuit onto the floor which Tom dutifully scrabbled to retrieve from under an antique table. I nibbled a cucumber sandwich with my granddaughter firmly wedged on one knee.

Before the occasion could deteriorate further, I drank half a cup of Earl Grey which I detest, thanked the host for her hospitality and muttered apologies before taking Olivia home. Black marks for both of us that day and we've never been invited to the lodge since. I have on several occasions, invited my mother-in-law to Sunday lunch at the Hall, but she churlishly declines to join us for Christmas. Too many memories lie within, apparently, and I quietly celebrate my good fortune. Tom dutifully visits her on

Christmas morning and accompanies her to matins. Then he's all ours for the remainder of the day.

I oversee the daily stream of visitors and the bevy of attractions we've created to part them from their money. We're blessed with good staff for the café which serves homemade delights created on site by the indomitable Eileen. I need to be strong around her feather-light Victoria sandwiches and the homemade fudge is a forbidden fruit.

A local lady called Grace was found to help with Olivia, and not only is she flexible about her hours, but she is much admired by our granddaughter. Even though Olivia is now at school, we're able to employ Grace elsewhere on the estate until the school holidays come around. All appears to be back on an even keel for the family and I'm more than grateful for that.

My daughter is a Judas... well, that's how it feels. I'm more furious than I've ever felt in my life. Anger is sitting like a metal coil in my chest and those night elves have come back to torment. I was convinced Olivia would soon be ours. How can Saskie drop this on us after all we've done for her? Olivia feels like our own and that's partly due to the lack of interest her mother has shown in her wellbeing.

Saskia gave me a load of crap when I challenged her decision to give her daughter away. She denied she was 'giving her away' and tried to tell me Olivia needed to live with the only blood relative who wanted her. Apparently, we don't count on that front. It's Saskia's intention to permanently bow out of her daughter's life to pursue the life she wants, which doesn't include a child. But how can it be better for Olivia to live with a man who is at best, a ruffian?

I'm not good when life gets beyond my control as I'm a Capricorn and I need to know what's happening and why. Sadly, I'm unable to submerge hostile thoughts about my daughter who has never regained her closeness to me since the coma. But how could she do this to us? Tom and I are determined she won't get away with it, although we're not fighting for ourselves, but to protect Olivia's best interests. How can it be better for her to be dragged from the only home she's known to stay with a family living on the breadline?

It looks as if we are going to meet bloody Alfie Collins in court again. Our solicitor thinks we have a good case and that Olivia's best interest is served by her staying with us. But it's what the judge decides that really matters. I'm strong as a bulldog about this and there will be none of the wishy-washy Lottie, as seen when Saskia was ill. I know we're going to win.

Because I am so angry with my daughter we are out of contact at the moment, although I noticed her allowance is still dropping into her bank account. It's usual for her to come home at Easter but I can't find it in my heart to invite her and Nate to stay this year. It feels hypocritical and sad in equal measure. And does Olivia need to gobble her Easter bunnies with a mother who is about to abandon her? I don't think so.

Heidi Brooker rang me yesterday and as usual, she can always lighten anyone's mood. She told me all the gossip from Churchill's including details of the new Head of Art who has a pierced nose and a boy who has announced he's gay. OMG. Neither of us can believe either will be accepted by the establishment and we certainly had a giggle.

Heidi talks a lot of sense, and she came up with a good idea to help us gain custody of Olivia. I'm not sure Tom is keen, but he agreed that anything is worth a try. As I know too well, his quiet manner hides deep waters and I think he fears Alfie may win custody of his daughter if it goes to court, especially now he's turned his life around. The family appear to have come into some money, and they now look on the respectable side of rough, which Tom feels may bias the court case in their favour.

So, my friend Heidi is the reason I'm outside a block of housing association flats on the outskirts of Oxford; I have a dry mouth but spade loads of confidence. I also have a list of incentives which I'll offer one by one, until I make a breakthrough with our plans. This has to work.

The grubby door is opened by the same mousey woman who sat on the end of the row at the court case five years ago. The one I noticed crying. She's petite and looks good enough without makeup. I see from her face that she knows who I am.

''Spose you'd better come in.'

I thank her and enter a neat, almost tasteful sitting room with photos of Olivia and an older girl displayed in various vantage points. That feels bloody strange and for one minute I slide off-piste. But I gather myself together and sit where indicated by the almost shy lady who is clearly surprised to find me on her doorstep.

'I've come about Olivia, which I'm sure you've guessed.'

I get no reaction but give silence a chance to develop into something verbal. It doesn't, so I take the initiative. 'It's about the custody... the court case.... My husband and I wondered....'

''Spose *you* want to keep her.'

I didn't expect such bluntness, but I agreed that was why I'd come.

'My Alfie is dead set on getting her. He's her dad, so she should be with him. Seeing as her mother don't want her.'

'Ouch. But I remember my arguments. 'We are her stability... we're all she's known. I've brought her up from the time she was born. I even fought to ensure she wasn't aborted. I think I have a good case to keep her too.'

Tracey slid her hair behind her ears and I thought how young she looked. I nodded to the photos....' Is that your daughter with Olivia?'

'Yeh. Dead proud of my Lily, I am.'

'How old is she?'

'Thirteen, going on twenty-four!'

'I know what a handful teenage girls can be. Saskia was never easy and when the problem with drugs and the coma hit our family, I was devastated that I hadn't been able to keep her safe. That's what mothers want, isn't it? To keep their children safe?'

Tracey looked at me and I could see she was softening. I could see a glimmer of sympathy. 'The thing is Tracey, I wondered if you could persuade Alfie to come to an agreement whereby we kept Olivia but he has generous access. That way she'd have all of us in her life.'

'My Alfie thinks he'll win her in court.'

'But it isn't about winning is it? It's about what's best for Olivia.'

Tracey appears to digest my thoughts for a few minutes while I soak up the silence.

'But I was going to help with her. You know, pick her up from school and things.'

'I think Olivia would hate to change schools. She's really settled and...

'Think our schools aren't good enough?'

'Tracey, this isn't a contest. This is real life for Olivia and all of us want the best for her. How can taking her from us at the age of five and plonking her into a different family be good for her?'

'You mean she's better off in a posh family than living with the likes of us?'

'I didn't come here to fight. I came here to avoid a fight in court. It's bound to get brutal, and haven't we all been hurt enough?'

'How much access was you thinking?'

'How much do you think would be fair?'

She thought for a minute or two. 'Every other weekend and taking her on holiday each year. Not sure what Alfie would say but...'

'Why don't you try it? We'd pay for everything she needs. Her clothes and any school bits and pieces.'

For some reason Tracey looked at her watch and the talking was over.

'I'll think about it. Give me yer phone number and I'll think about it.'

'Thank you. I can't ask for more than that.' I wrote our telephone number on a piece of paper she gave me and before I could say another word I was out of the door, wondering what I'd said to be ousted so abruptly.

And then I realised. Alfie was locking his car as I got into mine and it had been a close-run thing if she didn't want Alfie to know I'd visited.

It wasn't going to be easy to keep our granddaughter. It felt like the second time I'd fought for her life and this time I was wading through treacle. Tracey and I met several times and at each meeting, I thought the atmosphere warmed a little. I got her around to agreeing what was best for Olivia, although relaxation of access was essential if we had any hope of keeping her. I reasoned that having some of my little girl was better than losing her to Alfie. Of course, I'd given no thought to Saskia's views on this, but I wanted an agreement from the Collins family before I approached my daughter.

I reasoned that if Alfie's bid to have Olivia was dropped, then Saskia would obviously want to leave her with Tom and me. Once more I was walking on eggshells, but I'd do anything to keep that little girl. After negotiating further, Tracey went to work on her son. Inevitably, I had to meet with him, and he was reluctant to agree with our plans, but made the point that when she was older she could choose where she lived. I agreed, having no doubt about where that would be.

The outcome of my agreement with the Collins family inevitably caused heartache. Alfie bargained hard when it went down to the wire, and I capitulated to the point where he has Olivia for half of all school holidays as well as every other weekend. I did make a proviso that if Olivia, for any reason, did not want to visit her father, then I would not force her. I hoped I'd covered all bases. Tracey did a great job and I'll forever be grateful to her for persuading her son to find a middle way that was best for his daughter. I was allergic to any more fighting and happier to have found a compromise.

I asked Alfie to let Saskia know about his decision. I knew it was cowardly, but they were making life-changing decisions about their child, so it seemed right. Quite how he gave her the information I have no idea, but Saskia left a putrid answerphone message to say she wanted nothing more to do with us. Her parting shot was that we couldn't adopt Olivia although she could stay with us for the 'foreseeable future.'

I pine for the loss of my daughter and hope my granddaughter will never make me regret the sacrifice. Tom promised me Saskia would calm down, and maybe she will, but the chasm inside me is deep. Why does life have to be so complicated?

And so, a five-year-old little girl is taking the changes to her life with little resistance. Olivia finds Lily a big attraction when she visits her father, and they go the extra mile to do things that please her. I wonder how long that can last and hope they fall into a more manageable routine. Next Christmas it's already agreed that Olivia will be with the Collins family and if we have no breakthrough with Saskia, then we will be a lonely twosome for the festive season. In my quiet moments, I convince myself that life is so much richer with Olivia in it than if she'd been aborted. I firmly believe I made the right decision although Tom would probably not agree since the fallout. He thinks one child has been sacrificed for the other. Brutal.

I involve myself in the business, which is busier than ever, and I try not to overthink the problems. Tom argues that we had the best deal possible, in view of Saskia's insistence that Alfie remained in Olivia's life. He even told me I'd done an excellent job of keeping Olivia with us; he knows he could never have negotiated with Alfie.

So here we are. Our daughter, who is not speaking to us, still manages to convey her need for money. Saskia always contacts Tom for her needs as I suspect she finds it impossible to deal with my misery and anger. She knows me well and I can't help thinking of the early years when our heartbeats were as one. I'm going to leave it another couple of months and then I shall contact Nate. Maybe he can provide a sliver of hope for reconciliation.

Every Easter and summer, Saskia has worked on the estate to earn money for her life in Exeter. We, of course, pay all her tuition fees but the additional needs surrounding a medical degree are substantial. She's made no attempt to come home, and Easter has already been and gone.

It was a June day, just a few weeks ago, when the telephone intruded as I was restocking the cake stand for Eileen. My stomach flipped as I recognised Saskia's voice.

'Mum... Mummy I....'

'What is it, darling. I can't hear you through the tears. Come on, it can't be so bad. We can sort anything together.'

'Yes, but I've been such a cow to you and Daddy... I...'

'Yes but you're our own special cow, aren't you?'

I heard a stifled laugh through the tears.

'Can we come home next weekend? Me and Nate?' I stifled the desire to correct her grammar. 'You never need to ask, honey. Of course you can.'

'I'm so sorry Mummy. Really sorry.... Do you forgive me?'

'Shh... come home and we'll sort it all out. Olivia will be thrilled to see you.'

'Okay. Would you do roast pork on Sunday?'

'Of course, darling. Just drive carefully. Big hugs to you both.'

I'm fixating on roasting the pork. Not dreaming of what Saskia might say or any news she may have. I'm concentrating only on what I know, which is our daughter is coming home.

\*\*\*

Printed in Great Britain
by Amazon

51715137R00139